# HASAN

## A Novel

Drew Saunders

Glendower Media
11850 Whitmore Lake Rd Ste A
Whitmore Lake, Michigan 48189
**www.glendowermedia.com**

# DEDICATION

I started writing this book in 2011, when I heard about the death of **Hamza Al Khateeb**. Hamza was a Syrian teenager caught in between the protests that started the war in Syria and the Draconian security forces that tortured and ultimately murdered him. This book is dedicated to him. Although Hasan is not supposed to be him, nor do I pretend to be at all close to him or his family, he is the reason I started writing. I finished reading the article, I think on the BBC's web site, and sat there in my room -- angry. I tried to process it for five minutes or so and couldn't, so I started writing. The first chapter of this book was the result. I didn't take inspiration nor base any part of the book on Hamza's tragic story. I just took his generation's situation and used my imagination. Although, if I had my way, I would have rather not written this book if Hamza, and the generation of Syrian millennial like him, could have grown up like me -- where war zones are confined to the news and video games.

# CONTENTS

# Chapter One
# My Name is Hasan

My name is Hasan. I'm fifteen. I was born in Damascus but moved to Homs when I was two when my father got promoted. I had been sitting on the floor of my kitchen, for I don't know how long, staring at the door which led to the hallway. I leaned my head against the edge of the counter. I couldn't come to grips with the wreck my house was. Everything had been destroyed -- including me.

"Hasan, I'm bored. Let's go."

My little sister, Ishtar (Star), was ten. We called her Ish. She was sort of stringy, with hazel eyes and slightly mousy hair. And she was certain she was beautiful. She was Dad's favorite. And she knew it.

"Sit back down." I said.
"No."
"Ish." I said, testily.
"You're not the boss of me."

I hit my head in frustration. The room we were in used to be our kitchen. After the army shelled the city, the dirt and the soot stayed in the air for hours, falling on everything like mist in a rainy forest.

"Who's the oldest one here?" I asked with my eyes closed.
"Hasan." She said, shortly.
"Who's the oldest family member in this room?"
"You are."
"And what has Dad always said when neither parent is there?"
"We don't know he's not here."
"He is not here. He's gone."
"Gone where exactly?"
"Somewhere else."

"I know what 'gone'... "

"What has Dad always said when he and Mom aren't there?"

"The oldest sibling is in charge."

"What did Mom always say?"

"That when Mom and Dad aren't there, the oldest sibling is in charge."

"Fantastic," I said. "Now shut up."

She was about to open her mouth to retort when Asu spoke. "I'm scared."

My little brother, Asu (The East), is nearly five. Ever since he could walk, Asu has been following me around whether I wanted him to or not. He's been staying closer these last few months. "I know," I said and rubbed his head in an awkward way, not really touching him much. "Just stay tough for me and....."

I didn't really finish that sentence. I was scared to and not confident at all I would be able to get them out of Homs alive. There was dirt everywhere. There was blood. There were bodies. I didn't want to lie to him.

And I didn't feel like I should. Apart from the war not having to happen, I hated how it had. I hated Assad for not giving into the protestors. He could have just resigned like the Tunisian guy did -- I forgot his name. I hated the protestors for demanding reforms to democracy in the first place. I hated Egypt because their revolution worked and ours, at least so far, didn't.

But then I took that back in my head. They had gotten rid of their dictator and they had had elections. But then they had a billion coups. Not much to envy there.

I hated the extremists who took advantage of the chaos to turn Syria into a shooting gallery. I hated being alone. And I hated being in charge of these two. I could have left them behind. But I hated my conscience, weighing me down like an anchor. I couldn't just leave them.

I have lived here in Homs all my life. But I couldn't recognize it now. My street, my neighbors, my mosque, my house, my life. And yes, my family.

"Are you hungry?" Ish asked Asu.

"Mm-hmm."

"Well," Ish said, gesturing to herself in what I think she thought was grown up way, "I would love to go get you some food. But *someone* won't let me!"

"Boom!" I said, sarcastically, with my fingers. "And Ish has unlocked a new bitchy level. Master. Fifty bonus levels."

"You're so funny." Ish said and stood up.

"I *am* hungry Hasan." Asu said.

"Working on it."

"Are they going to start shelling again?"

"I don't know."

Asu was very good at making that wounded puppy whimpering noise. I looked at him.

"Listen, I …"

I heard a board creak. I looked up and saw Ish walking to the hallway.

"Ish, stay here!" I shouted with a start.

"Why?" Ish whined as she turned around in the door frame.

I didn't answer that. I just gave her my well-practiced, *"What do you think?"* Look.

She huffed and sat back down next to me. "We can't stay here forever."

To be honest, at first I couldn't think past getting out of Mom's closet where I had been with Ish and Asu. Back when the shelling first started, Dad had taken all of us to his bedroom and put us in the closet.

"Hasan, don't let them out, and take care of them till I come back! I am going to look for a safe way out." He shut the door and left. A few hours later I took Ish and Asu down to the kitchen.

"When Daddy finds out you're being mean to me you're going to be in big trouble! You're going to be grounded!" Ish said.

I would have killed to get grounded again. But Dad couldn't ground me. You see, he was dead.

# Chapter Two
## It Started

It started for me when the shelling began. I guess for everyone else it started in Tunisia. My brother was really into the protests when they started.

Like everywhere else in the Arab World, from Morocco to Oman, things had changed. Just a few years ago the very idea of protesting in a crowd against Al Assad was laughable.

Then a man in Tunisia set himself on fire, partly in protest to his local dictator's government. The resulting protests led that dictator to resign and flee the country. That caused a domino effect across North Africa to the Middle East.

Most people wanted a democracy and they saw that it was not only attainable but it was happening. Everyone poured into the streets and protested civil rights style. And my brother Amir was right there with them. I went when I could and every time the crackdown by the police got rougher and rougher. Then they sent the military in.

The wash of the jets shook the whole neighborhood but at first I thought they were just flying past. By then Amir had already left. He was joining the rebels. We weren't sure where. As soon as the jet was out of range I heard something familiar.

Artillery fire.

It started for me when I was standing in front of my house, watching the jets come back. Dad was standing in the doorway, leaning against the frame.

Down the street, Mom was talking with friends. She was lucky to get out of the house to be honest. Ever since Amir left, Dad locked us all up in the house. He'd changed when the military came in. He became super protective. He barely left the house himself and he certainly wasn't going to let anyone else out.

It was like that for two weeks. But eventually, Mom and Dad argued for the last time. Mom won the argument. She reasoned that there was so much going on that it was just as dangerous at home as anywhere else. So Dad reluctantly allowed Mom to go out in a group-- a large group but not large enough to be a target.

The military had started using artillery to disperse the crowds. Then they started firing indiscriminately on neighborhoods. Like my neighborhood.

Afterwards, thugs hired by the Assad government would go through and loot. And then the military would come in like cavalry to claim they were defending us. Usually they would run into the real rebels who came in to actually protect civilians. That's what happened to my family.

I guess Mom was rooted to the spot. She saw the missile come down and from a block-and-a-half away. I could see her eyes widen. The six women she had gone out with all clutched to her for support, as if they were asking her what to do. She didn't answer them. She must've known it was too late. But then she broke out into a run anyway. She ran towards me. And then the missile hit.

Mom disappeared in an orange ball.

The wind was displaced so much that the wave it created washed over me like the snap of a whip and distorted the sound. At first there was no sound and then a deafening boom snapped over me. It broke out all of the windows.

Now *I* was rooted to the spot. I didn't feel anything. I just kept replaying in my head what just happened. The artillery started firing. I could hear it miles away. Dad grabbed me from behind by my collar and half-ran/half-dragged me back into the house.

"Hasan!" Asu said and poked me and I was shaken back into reality.

"What?" I snapped at him.

"What're we gonna do now?"

Ever since Asu could talk, he's been asking me that same stupid question. "What're we gonna do now?" Pain in the ass. And of course, all Mom ever did was put me in charge of him. I'd ask her, "Why can't Ish do it?" Usually she'd say because I was in charge of her too.

"I don't know." I snapped.

"I want to go back to the living room." Ish said.

"Stay. Put." I said.

I didn't know what I was going to do next. I just know that Ish and Asu were never, ever going back into that living room. I didn't want them to see what was in there.

"There are people out there." Ish said, pointing out the window.

"You're right." said Asu.

A cluster of five people were shuffling along the wall on the other side of the small square by my house. They came to a door off-center from the middle of the square and knocked furiously quietly.

The door opened and a man with a machine gun hurried them in, practically shoving them inside. I recognized him immediately and so did Ish.

"That's Mr. Saiid!"

"Yep." I said.

"What's he doing?" Asu said, trying, to look through the window on his tippy toes.

He was failing so I held him up, "I think he's hiding people."

"He isn't being very nice." Ish decided out loud.

"What're you talking about?" I asked.

"He shoved that lady inside! Wait till I tell Dad!"

"What?"

"I said wait until I tell Dad."

"Ok. Asu, here's what we're going to do."

"What?" Asu came back to life.

"We're going to go through this window."

"Why can't we use the door?" Ish wondered.

"Because we can't."

"Why?" Asu asked.

"Because um…" It took me a minute to come up with a reason. "There's a lot of broken glass in the rest of the house."

"There's broken glass in here." Ish said.

"Yea well, there's none out there and Dad doesn't want one of you to stab your feet so he told me to take you out through the window."

"Cool." Asu said. He thinks all of my ideas are cool.

"How?" Ish said, "There are bars on the window."

"Oh yea," I looked around the kitchen, "Um…Here…"

I put Asu down and took one of the kitchen knives. I opened the window -- what was left of it -- and pushed the blade against the bars.

Man, they came off easily!

# Chapter Three
# The Hovel

When we got to the -- uh -- I don't know what to call it. It wasn't a camp. It wasn't a hide out. It was more of just a cluster of survivors. It was chaotic. We were in what used to be someone's living room. There was still a couch, a few lamps and side tables, and the split wood that was once a coffee table.

Before anyone had gotten there, a large piece of shrapnel had flown off the city streets and dropped though the squat building above us like a pebble through a damp few pieces of tissue paper. It hadn't done much actual damage, but it splattered on the ground and made a mess. Several men were trying to clear the rubbish out of the middle so more people could use it.

Squatting everywhere were about eight families and a dozen others in our two hundred and forty square foot room. The TV was split open in a corner. There was dirt on everything. There was staining on the carpet. Blood? Probably.

In the corner a male nurse, still in his scrubs, was in the middle of a makeshift surgery on a man who looked like he was in shock. He was lucky to be alive considering how little of his chest was still there.

I took Ish and Asu to the other side of the somewhat large room where the women had the children. They were all standing up, making themselves as big as possible and doing anything they could think of to make the children not look at the surgery. To be honest, I didn't see much of a point in what they were doing. Everyone had seen so many dead bodies, what was one more, really?

Ish came into the room from behind me and walked automatically to the group of women and kids and sat down. One of the mothers was busy doing a head-count of all the children. Her name was Amalia and seemed to know everybody in town. I've known her all my life. When Ish sat down she stopped counting, glanced up at me and shouted. "Hasan!"

She beckoned me and Asu over.

"Thank Allah that you're all right." She said and wiped some dirt off my face. I've always hated it when they do that. Mom did it, too. Or she used to.

Then I stopped myself. I wasn't thinking about her. I could handle Dad being dead. I didn't think I could handle her being dead. So I kicked her out of my mind. I decided that I could fall apart later. But only later.

"When the bombs started dropping and I saw your mother…"

She trailed off. Great. I almost got away with not thinking about Mom. Couldn't she realize that I didn't want to talk about it? I'll think about it years from now. I guess she didn't want to think about her either. She and Mom were friends. She changed the subject.

"Well, at least you're all right." She turned to Asu. "You hungry Asu? We've got food. Mr. Saiid was thoughtful enough to bring an armful of bread after the bakery was abandoned."

Asu smiled, sort of, and let go of my hand. He let Amalia take him over to the other kids. They were all like Ish and Asu. Kids from just babies to my age, all huddled in the corner. The women were all standing in the middle of the room, doing their best to keep them from seeing what was going on behind them. Like they couldn't hear it.

I decided that the guy they were trying to save wasn't going to make it. And I could tell by the look on the nurse's face that he didn't think he would either. But he was still trying anyway. The women seemed to have forgotten about me for the moment. I wondered why.

Mom used to say I was mature for my age. But I assumed that all mothers liked to say that about their sons. Did Amalia and the other women think so too? I thought about it and glanced up.

I could see a sort of tunnel to the sky where the big piece of shrapnel had hit the building. I could see the opening funnel up to the sky. It was blue, but there was a white cloud going by it. It blocked the sun for a minute and it got a little bit dark in the hovel.

"Hey Hasan!"

I turned around and a stocky, green eyed kid with ripped jeans and a yellow t-shirt came up and hugged me. I frankly hadn't expected Abdullah to be still alive. I've known him all my life and he was always the kid who got every answer wrong, tripped in the hallway, lost everything and was picked last at every sport. He had ADHD.

"Thank Allah you're alive!"
"I can't believe it!"
"Is it just you or ...?"
"My brother and sister are with me."
"Nobody else?"
"No."
"I'm alone."
"You -- you are?"
"Ya."
"I'm sorry."
"I'm not worried yet. I mean, I am, but - "
"Hasan!", two other people exclaimed. A boy and a girl, also my age, ran up and stopped just short of hugging me.
"Dude, how are you still alive?" The guy said, "I saw them raid your house!"
"Are you hurt?" The girl said.

Mohammad was six months younger than me. A preppy, lean kid with ear lobes the size of my big toes and was from one of the only Shia families in my mostly Sunni neighborhood.

His sister, Fatma, looked nothing like her normal self. She was the happiest, peppiest girl I have ever met and was always happy to see everybody, to help anyone, and to chat with anyone, especially college girls. Especially about boys. She was always smiling. And to see her now, not smiling -- was jarring.

"I'm fine. We're fine."
"Our parents got us out last night. We made it about six kilometers north and then we ran out of gas. None of the stations have power and the ones using generators were so clogged with

lines that we just didn't try."

The irony of running out of gas in a part of the world so full of oil was not lost on me.

"We were going to just walk north but then the army cut us off, so we had to come back."

"Or it might've been one of Assad's militias. Or some extremist group. We're not sure. We didn't see them up close."

"Either way, here we are."

"You made it back that easy?" I asked.

The sound of their escape made me feel overly optimistic. If they could get in and out, then maybe Dad's stupid idea, the only plan I had so far, wasn't such a bad idea after all.

"Well, Tasnia got shot."

Tasnia was Fatma's best friend. A Sunni girl light in skin, height, hair and brains, she had been telling everyone at school and the mosque I went to with her that she was going to be a model on the runways of Paris. And she said that right up until she got to high school, when she decided she would design the clothes instead.

But she was shot? Judging by "shot" I presumed she was still alive, but for a girl like her, if she was hit anywhere close to the face, she may as well not be.

"She was grazed in the arm. She's fine." Fatma said.

The tone of her voice stuck with me. She was scared, like the rest of us, but defiant. As if she was telling the world how her friend was fine, and how she would pull through it, or else. I guess her coping mechanism was to just defy her way through it, no matter how many bullets whizzed through her hair.

Asu's coping mechanism, as usual, was to tug on the back of my button-down shirt. I turned around and spat, "What?"

"Asu!" Fatma nearly shrieked, suddenly delighted.

She scooped Asu up and kissed his cheek. He hung onto

her side and looked at me and Mohammad, who said, "You ok, Asu?"

Mohamed asked Asu if he was going to help him go to Damascus to bring the fight to Assad. I stopped him in his tracks. I had gotten Asu this far without him dying; I wasn't going to let him start thinking he was going on some sort of quest to Damascus. Most of the time he was in the corner cowering and afraid. If that kept him from running off and getting killed in the cross fire or the shock-wave of a bomb, then that's how I wanted him for the time being-- as long as he got up and moved when I wanted him to.

The conversation ended when Fatma took Asu away to the others, and Mohammad took me over to a corner where nobody was.

"Dude, did you see the look in Saiid's eye when you came in here."

"Yea, I did."

"He's changed, to say the least."

"He's bossier than ever."

"He's like a sheep dog."

"Because he's herding everybody?"

"Everybody he can find. And while that's a good idea, I don't think it's a good idea."

"Why?"

"We're more of a target, one. We have more people to keep track of, two. And three, we don't have enough guns, to say nothing of ammo."

"Do you think the Americans will come?"

Mohammed shook his head. His earlobes shook with him like ear rings.

"I don't think so."

"Do you want them here?"

"I dunno. If they stopped it, I guess."

"It's not that I don't want them. I just don't think they want to be here."

"Why not? All our lives they've talked over and over about

expanding democracy. Why not help us when we're trying to do that now?"

"Hey, Mohammed!" Abdulla ran over.

"Hey, are you alright?" Mohammed asked.

"Yes. Praise Allah you're ok."

"Yea. What're you guys talking about?"

"Nothing."

"Really dude; it's nothing." I said.

I liked Abdulla. I really did. But he was a klutz, to put it nicely. I didn't think he was stupid, or a coward or anything. But he was the most ADHD person in the country with butter fingers. Nobody in their right mind would put a gun in his hand. And that is exactly what Saiid did.

I have no idea where the AK- 47s came from but suddenly I had one, Mohammed had one, Abdulla had one and every able-bodied man or teenaged guy had one. And some of the more formidable women. We had lots of guns but a noticeably tiny amount of ammunition. We got three clips each.

"If we get in a fight, this ammo isn't going to last." I said.

"This thing's going to slip right out of my hands isn't it?" Abdulla said.

"You'll be fine." Mohammed lied. "Just stick with us, ok? Saiid said it first. He needs every adult with a brain and somewhat of an aim."

"I've never fired a gun before in my life." Abdulla said.

"Neither have I." I said.

"I haven't either. But I guess we'll learn how."

"Ok." Abdulla said and breathed purposefully out of his nostrils. "Ok."

We were quiet for a minute, looking at each other.

"Now what?" I finally asked.

"Now you come up with a plan or something and take over being the guy with balls. I need a breather."

"I say we just wait until Saiid comes up with a plan. I don' "

I don't know what I was going to say next. They brought Tasnia in. The guy the nurse had been trying to save in the corner was long dead. The nurse hopped up from the arm of the couch he was sitting on, dropped his cigarette and helped bring Tasnia in. Fatma also helped. We watched in the corner as Fatma, who wanted to be a doctor anyway, got a crash course in changing a bandage.

"Ok," The nurse said. "Looks like the wound's not doing that bad, considering. We need to wash it. I'll do that, and disinfect. Then you're going to learn how to wrap."
"Right."

And from the couch, the three of us watched them slowly and carefully replace Tasnia's bandage. Amelia held Tasnia's unconscious hand.

"Shame on them," Amelia said, "I saw the video of the car you were in. They knew perfectly well you were in the car. They obviously did! Wait 'til I get my hands on one of them."

Fatma turned out to be a natural, and that look in her eye, the kind of intensity that stabbed through you like a needle, stayed steady. I doubt she'll ever be the same again. She wasn't fazed when Saiid and a second man marched into the room. I looked up and almost successfully suppressed a gasp.

For a second, I would have sworn it was our brother - Amir. After we saw a protest on the news, and our sister Aisha might have died, that was it for him. He had been talking about going and joining the resistance ever since the protests had started coming east from Tunisia. Dad told him no, that he wanted to keep the family in one place. But after we saw that video, I knew he would disappear.

For a second, I thought that this guy with Saiid was Amir. He looked just like him. Tall, handsome, leanly muscular, with the slightest hint of stubble around his chin and a slightly upturned nose. But it wasn't him. It was like one of those pictures which is exactly the same but with half a dozen deliberate mistakes.

"How's she doing?"
"Good." The nurse said. "Really good."

Saiid ignored her from then on.

"How much food do you have left?" he asked Amelia.
"Not much," she said.
"I've sent two men out to get more. Don't know how much they'll get but it'll have to do."
"That's fine, I... "
"Boys, on your feet."

We stood up.

"To get food and supplies, I've had to thin our perimeter." He chucked his head once to the Guy Who Looked Like Amir, "He's going to take you one by one to the corners that need the most muscle. One of you per position. When you get there, do whatever the guy already there tells you to."
"Wait just a second! They're just boys! You can't send them out there."
"Shut up Amelia."
"Nobody put you in charge you know."
"Nobody put you in charge, now shut up."
"Who died and made you Assad?"
"That can't possibly be your best come back."

It went on like that for a while. When adults argue, they're "having a discussion." When I do it or when Amir does it or when Mohammed or Fatma or Abdulla do it, we're behaving like kids. It lasted long enough for the guys he sent to come back with some of the food and none of the ammo that they had promised.
Saiid chewed them out for not getting the ammo while Amelia thanked them for the food. Saiid reassigned them back to their positions and forgot about us entirely. At one point, Ish marched right up to me with her share of week-old food.

"Eat it." She said.
"You eat it."

15

"You haven't eaten since yesterday and Mom's not here, so now it's my job to make you eat. Now eat!"

I smiled a bit, too hungry to argue with her. So I ate it.

"Thanks."
"You're welcome."

I was midway through a bite when she asked me what she came over to say.

"Hasan, are Amir and Aisha over where Dad is?"
I swallowed. "I dunno, maybe."
"Before she died...........Mom was adamant that Aisha was ok, that she was safe."
"Uh-huh."
"You think Dad found her, and took her to Lebanon? Or that Amir did?"
"That's what he said he'd do, or something like that."
"I hope she's there."
"Yea -- me too."

Bang!

The whole room shrieked and hit the deck, most of them landing on their knees or someone else. What was distinctly a sniper rifle had just fired and the bullet hit something. And that something, we were all pretty sure, was the wall to this room.

Ish and Asu ran into me like rugby players tackling the other team. I squatted and dragged them down with me to make us less of a target. Saiid had the whole room lie on the floor. He went out with a few other fighters to see what was happening. I squeezed my eyes shut and ransacked my mind for something, anything, to take me away from there.

# Chapter Four
# Aisha

What I found was Aisha. Aisha had left for college in Damascus six months before all the troubles happened. My brother Amir and I felt totally differently when my sister left. While she had lived at home, she bumped heads with Amir on just about everything.

When she left, I could tell, he took it hard. But he didn't want to talk to anybody about it. My mother was shaken, but only cried when she thought nobody could see her. However, our old house was built like an old cardboard box. There were holes, tiny ones, in every corner. It was easy to hear what's going on in any room. Dad was shaken, but he always had been stern and overbearing. The few times he did emote was to Mom, and only then when they were alone and out of the house. Ish and Asu were too young to understand.

Even though they watched the protests on TV with us, they didn't get it. The day when Al Assad came on the TV and announced that a new constitution was in effect my parents, Amir and me looked at one another in disbelief.

What constitution?

Al Assad said that ninety percent of the population had voted for it.

What vote?

He was cheered on by a bunch of people off- camera. Father shook his head silently. Mother rolled her eyes and then looked at Asu. When Asu wasn't bothering me, he bothered Mother. So she watched him jabber on about who knows what while some commercials played.

I brought in a tray of tea. Amir took one and added a huge amount of sugar to it. Father took two and handed one to mom. Then the reporter came on. Let me translate for him.

He claimed that there was another uprising in Damascus, which means a protest was attacked by the army, and that the terrorists (civilian protesters)had been dispersed.

Seven of the terrorists (protesters) had been killed and

twenty arrested. As they broadcast this, they showed live footage of the army sweeping into a group of people. Mother looked at the screen and yelped, Amir gasped, father choked on his tea.

What we saw was a cluster of a dozen people. It was hard to tell exactly how they looked. Scared? Yes. But also angry. And determined, maybe brave. One of them was Aisha.

She was in a crowd of protestors in front of the cameras. To the side, a group of police marched towards them with their weapons raised. They fired.

She was covered in blood, screaming. She and a middle aged man were holding a man who had been shot. There was blood on all three of them. The image was on the screen for a second, no longer.

I shut out the world and closed my eyes, trying to recreate what I saw. A lot of the blood was certainly from the wounded young man. But was she hurt? Did she actually have a wound on her? Maybe. It happened so fast I'm not sure what I saw. Damn it. What happened to her? That's a question we've been asking over and over now for a month.

# Chapter Five
# Sniper

Bang!

Nobody moved. It's too far off.

Bang!

That one was closer.

Bang!

That last bullet hit the wall. He definitely knew we were in there. Ish shifted closer to me. Asu practically crawled into my lap. At one of the two doors, a little girl tried to run out but was grabbed around the waist at the last second by her mom who was wearing a full burka, with her face covered so I couldn't see it. But I don't have to. Her eyes registered terror when she saw her daughter's legs move. We're trapped in here.

Bang!

Tasnia woke up after the third shot. She jerked to life in one of the corners. When she did her head snapped up and she went into a lying position on her elbows, a few inches above Fatma's lap where her head had been resting. Fatma and Abdullah were whispering over each other, trying to keep her calm and quiet. That only worked after another…

Bang!

It took a while but they got her to calm down. But it was still loud in here. Gunshots aside, there was a white noise in the room. Breathing.

People were panting like dogs at a race track from exhaustion as much as fear. Looking back, I don't know why we didn't just leave the building. I guess it was because this was the first safe place we had. We didn't just not want to leave. I think we didn't think we could find anything as remotely safe as this again.

Bang!

I could see why they chose this room. It was windowless, in the middle of the building. There used to be rooms around it on three sides, but they had caved in. The rubble now acted as a sort of armor, ricocheting bullets away from us.

Bang!

That bullet was closer to the corner. There was one wall that didn't have any rubble around it. Could his bullets make it through the wall with no rubble there? I didn't want to find out.

Bang!

That was even closer to the corner. He must have changed positions. The sniper must be on a rooftop across the boulevard.

He was probably squatting close to the roof, moving sideways with a crawl, keeping the building in his sights.

If he made it to the exposed wall, and I can't see why he couldn't, it would be like sticking a pencil through a sheet of paper. But on the wall opposite the one where he first started firing at, there were the doors. If he was moving to the exposed wall, we should get out now. I was about to suggest this when –

"On your feet everyone!" It was Saiid again. He was out of breath and his AK-47 is dangling by the strap on his arm, which was grabbing the door frame. "We need to get you downstairs. That wall isn't strong enough! Come on!"

We broke the land speed record on the way out of there. I was behind Abdullah, Mohammed and Fatma, who were carrying Tasnia. There was a jam at the doors but I got out with Ish holding my hand. Behind me was Asu. I turned around. Asu was gone.

"Where's your brother?" I shouted at Ish.
"I don't know." She said honestly.

I looked over my shoulder and realized immediately what had happened. Letting go of Ish's hand, I tried to force my way back into the room. But a torrent of survivors was pushing the other way and I barely made it two yards. Ish was one of many people yelling behind me. It was really loud. But I heard her say,

"Hasan! Come back! Come back!"

I think she was the only one in the room who wasn't crying besides me. I was too focused on finding Asu. I kept elbowing my way through the constant stream of mothers carrying already frazzled infants down to the basement and men with rifles and the injured.

Over the noise Saiid said, "Nobody panic! Just get into the cellar!"

Eventually, Asu ran into my legs. He'd gotten scared when I was separated from him and was crying. I picked him up without preamble and reversed course. I shifted him to one of my arms and slowed down only briefly to pick up Ish with my other arm and carry them down the narrow and noticeably steep staircase.

As I'd said, three sides of the building had been destroyed in the massacre, mostly from the artillery bombardment. The outer wall of the staircase had been hit directly, and the bits hanging there looked like they would drop from the steel mesh wires at any second. It was as if someone had crushed a pop tart and dropped the pieces in the alley, but a few pieces were held up by the steel mesh. I slid to a stop behind Tasnia.

The wall was exposed to the square outside where the sniper was set up. It wasn't directly exposed to his cross hairs, but enough of it was open to make me sure that the sniper would see me and kill all three of us in a single shot.

"Keep going!" Saiid said as he shoved me. "Stay along

there!"

"You going to go?" I asked my friends.
"No way!" Fatma said.

Other people were going down the selected route despite the danger. I didn't exactly think before acting. My gut just said that if I stayed there we would definitely die. But if we kept going we'd only probably die. So I left the four of them to hide in a door frame next to the door and took Ish and Asu with me.

Saiid and another guy with an AK-47 shepherded me and several others along a route which they hoped would be less exposed. The staircase went down a third of the way, turned and went down another third of the way to what used to be the outside wall, then down another third to where the next floor was and it had a square void in the middle, where a railing used to be. The railing was gone. We had to stay as close as possible to the void without falling down the three floors to the basement cellar, but close enough to be in view of the wall for the shortest amount of time. There was no safer way. Once we were down the first third of stairs, hugging the wall tightly, we turned to the second tier of stairs. On the third time, the sniper figured out what we were doing and fired again.

Bang!

The guy who was with Saiid was behind the group and stopped at the wall. He put his back to it for a moment and then aimed around the corner and unloaded his entire clip in the sniper's general direction. I finally made it downstairs with both kids alive.

The cellar was tiny and people were still trying to shove in. But it was like trying to shove another shirt in a drawer that was simply too full. I stopped on the landing and debated going back or just staying there. Every adult I could see was thinking the same thing. They knew that they couldn't get in there but they weren't sure what else to do. We could still hear the sniper above us.

Bang!

Bang!

I looked back upstairs just in time to see the guy who stayed behind to fight get hit with a bullet and fall. It wasn't like seeing it in the movies. The bullet hit him in the chest like a paint ball and it spun him around. He landed on his shoulder and laid there. He didn't scream. There wasn't much blood. It was just like swatting a fly.

Tasnia had gotten on her feet while I was going downstairs. I didn't hear them decide to come downstairs but I think that is what they did. It was chaotic. But Tasnia was hurrying downstairs between Mohammed and Abdullah and Fatima.

The second bullet hit her in the chest and she flattened against the stairs. Fatma, who had been helping her from behind, lost balance and fell on her face. Mohammed and Abdullah picked her up before she even fell all the way and dragged her with them into the first corner of the landing of the stairs.

Fatma, Mohammed and Abdullah were trying to make themselves harder targets in their semi-exposed corner. The area was barely big enough for one person to temporarily hide. I knew they weren't going to last long. But I was powerless to help them.

Saiid saw this and ran up along the wall. He looked down at his friend. I could see in his face that he knew his friend was dead. Then Saiid did something clever. He vaulted the final flight of stairs and nearly ran into Mrs. Amalia.

"Have you got your purse?"
"My purse! What? Why do you want that now?"
"Just let me see it!" Saiid said impatiently and almost ripped it from her hands.

It took a minute for him to find what he was looking for. Once he did, he ran up with it held in his free hand and stood where he'd been. It was only when he used it that I realized it was a woman's mirror. He used it to look around the corner and I could see his eyes widen a bit when he found where the sniper was. But then I saw him frown slightly when he realized there was nothing he could do without getting shot. Not with a sniper this good.

"Hey Saiid!" The Guy Who Looks Like Amir shouted from

above.

"Hey!..."

Bang! The sniper fired so I couldn't hear his name.

"We're down here."
"Is everyone ok?" he shouted from above. "Where's...?"
"Dead!"
"Where's the sniper?"
"I know where he is. Do you have a scope?"
"My buddy's got one."

Saiid explained where he was and the second rebel upstairs, who turned out to be the nurse, laid down at the top of the staircase, this time behind some rubble. It took him a few minutes.

Bang!

I guess the sniper saw the nurse lying down. I could see the bullet enter the stair well and hit something. A chunk of dry wall dived down-- quite a lot of it actually. Saiid covered his face. For a second, I thought that the nurse was hit. Then I heard another shot.

Bang!

The sniper who had been hunting us never fired again.

# Chapter 6
# Funeral

Funerals these days were the most dangerous thing you can do. It used to be that a funeral was off-limits. Worldwide. But Assad didn't seem to know that. No. He knew, he just didn't care. To his credit though, at least he didn't behead anyone on YouTube.

That's why half of the people in our little hovel were against holding a funeral the next day. I woke up in between Asu and someone I didn't know. I didn't remember falling asleep. I panicked for a moment because I didn't know where Ish was. But I found her almost immediately, asleep about two yards away from me.

I leaned back down into a sloping sitting position against the wall and let my breath out of my nose. It was so quiet I could hear the bugs swarming around the seven dead bodies we had left in another room.

We couldn't leave them outside because it would have been a tell-tale sign that we were in here. So Mohamed, me, and some fighter I didn't know took Tasnia back into the small, windowless room, which had been musty to begin with. Out of the way.

After everyone woke up Saiid, who I guess was the impromptu leader of our little group, announced that there was a funeral going on today. Saiid had been on the phone with people around town and evidently there were seven or so groups like ours collected together. They had all been attacked.

It was going to be a mass funeral, twenty-four people or more. And it kicked everyone into a flurry of noise.

I don't remember exactly what was said but just about half of the adults were against it and the other half wanted to go. "We can't go there! We'll be sitting ducks! We have kids! half of the room argued. "We've got to go! These were our neighbors! Besides, are you going to let him get away with this?" the other half argued back. I was too sore and groggy to have an opinion, or for once, to voice one. The kids were just scared and hungry.

"Ok! Ok! Ok!" Saiid shouted over everyone. They all shut up and listened to him. "Look -- I get it. You're tired, you're scared, and you're alone. We're alone. I get it. But like you said, we're sitting ducks out there. But we're sitting ducks here, too. Look at what happened last night. We cannot stay here.  I have a place in mind where we can go. But you've got to trust me, for no other reason than I'm still here, to take you there. I don't know if we're going to make it there. But we're definitely never going to make it staying here."

He pointed at the room with the bodies.

"And what about them? They're alone too now. Believe what you want. But Allah wouldn't want us to leave them there without a decent burial. And damn it, we're going to give them one! The place where the funeral will be held is on the way anyway and they've got to get there and they were our friends. So we're taking them. We'll do the funeral -- quickly -- on the way -- and then we'll be out of there. If you don't want to go, fine. But then you can't come with us. Good luck here. Because these guys are with me. And they're not staying to protect you."

Nobody spoke. Saiid was the tallest man in the room. Everyone looked at him for a minute and then went without saying a word to pack up their stuff.

Before we left, Saiid said to the group at the door, "If we're attacked… If something happens, I want everyone to do as I say. Those of you who can fight, fight. Everyone else, I want you to split up. Forty or fifty targets will be harder to hit than a single clod of us. But I want everyone to meet up back here. Ok? … Ok."

And we left.

Like before, Saiid strong-armed me into going, and Ish and Asu followed me out of the door and to the square like ducks following their mother. All of the children followed the women like that. The Guy Who Looked like Amir was in front of us with a group of three others with AK-47s, looking around at every open window.  There were a lot of open windows. And at every ledge, and we were surrounded by ledges. And around every corner. I was in the middle looking down them, too.

The bodies, wrapped in sheets, were carried on the shoulders of people in the middle of our group. I realized at one point that I must have been walking next to Tasnia's body because Fatma was helping to carrying her.

"Fatma."

She didn't respond or even look at me. She just kept staring into space and shuffling.

"Fatma."

She didn't answer. I had known Fatma all my life. But I had never known her to be quiet.

When we got to the funeral area, I didn't know what I was looking at for a minute. For a brief second, I thought someone had laid out rolls of bed sheets. But no, they were bodies. Rows and rows of bodies covered in white sheets to be buried.

Some of them were really small.
As small as Asu.
Smaller.

The square itself was about six hundred years old, on the edge of downtown. The storefronts where they sold soccer jerseys, TVs, food, just about anything.

Like most of Homs, I didn't recognize it now. Every window was broken in, the trees were uprooted, every wall was scarred with bullets and shrapnel from explosions. It stank, and every one of the six story buildings looked condemned. The only thing that was the same was the swarm of people. Normally it had flower beds and trees where people ate lunch and a constant swarm of vans, taxis and scooters gushed around the edge.

At the corner of one of the small roundabouts was a mosque, where the funeral would usually have been held. I liked that mosque. It was beautiful on the inside - navy blue with lines of gold and creamy white. But it was caved in like an egg shell now.

One of its three minarets was still standing.

How annoying. It wasn't just the ruined mosque that upset everyone. It was everything else. Nobody said it but you could taste it in the air. The world had gone to hell -- and with this one landmark gone, it was just one insult too many on too many injuries. As a result, the already shell shocked, melancholy crowd had a bit of an annoyed taste in their mouths. It was one thing too many.

Around me people shuffled around suspiciously. Every now and then, someone shrieked either in excitement for finding one of their friends alive or sadness for finding someone they knew dead. There were three vans idling with their engines running in the corner, white with big Red Cross badges on them. They were throwing out bundles wrapped in plastic with water, food, and first aid kits.

"Hasan!" Abdullah elbowed his way through the crowd towards me.

"Hey."

"I got one of the things from the Red Cross. Here".

He handed me a wrap of flat bread, which was pretty much cold gyro.

"Thank you." I was touched.

"Here's some for you guys, too."

"Thank you!" Ish and Asu said, smiling.

The Red Cross wasn't able to give out the food fast enough and I never got water. A few people around us eyed us with envy. I didn't blame them but didn't know when we'd get food again. It was the most awkward moment I could remember.

"The Red Cross guys are from Greece."

"I suddenly like Greece a lot more." I said. Although I didn't really have much of an opinion in any way about Greece before. "If I get out of here, that's where I'm taking them."

"Really?" A fleck of lamb flew out of his mouth.

"Well, maybe." I didn't mean that. I just said it. Still, Greece looked really good to me over the next few days.

"I'm going to Australia. My uncle's son goes to college

there. I know that my aunt and a few other people are living with him. If I make it there, I'm sure they'll let me stay."

"Good." I felt like I was being short with him but I didn't know what else to say. Besides, I couldn't stop looking at how much of a bowl we were in. The buildings around us were six to nine stories high. But I was honest when I said, "I hope you make it."

The day I first met Abdullah, we were five and he spent most of the day in class falling over, wiping his nose, crying and being picked last for soccer. Physically, he hadn't changed much. He was the last person I wanted to be with in a war zone. He was the kid who always got picked on. I didn't want him to be the first one to get killed.

"Mohammed yelled at me for talking about that. He said we should all stay and fight."

I shrugged.

"Hasan," Ish tugged my arm a bit. "When can we get out of here?"

"Soon I hope."

"What Saiid said -- I get it. But I feel really exposed out here."

"Me, too."

"Saiid said we'd get started at 11:15." Abdullah said.

"What time is it now?" Ish asked.

"Ten after." He said.

Asu didn't say anything. He just hugged my leg. I was about to say something when Saiid came out of nowhere.

"Hasan, where do you think you're going without your gun?"

He shoved it into my hands.

"Don't leave it next time. We're probably going to need it."

Then he walked away. I hated that thing. But I couldn't figure out what I felt about Saiid. He was bossing me around and I hated that. But I couldn't bring myself to argue with him. I think he knew he was taking a huge risk by participating in this funeral. I think he was afraid this would happen. I think what Saiid wanted was for everyone to stay alive. But that didn't mean he was going to turn his back on the people who were dead. Maybe that's why we were there.

I was surprised by how many people showed up at the funeral. When the funeral started, the bodies, wrapped in white sheets, were carried in the middle and people started praying. And crying. I started to feel nervous. I didn't pay attention to the funeral at all; I was looking at the ledges, the windows. Eventually I made up my mind. Setting the gun on the ground, carefully, I took Asu's hand and then Ish's and then I started to move back.

Back... ╱
Back...
Back.
Back.
Back.
Back.
Back.
Bang!

The ambush started with a sniper fire and then the militia moved in. It was like dropping a rock in a bucket of still water. Suddenly everything went haywire and I started running. I half-ran and half-dragged Asu and Ish out of there and down an alley. I had to sprint to keep from getting run over by what seemed like everyone in Syria running behind me.

People were yelling and falling all over the place. People stopped to help but were then either killed themselves or were trampled by the stampede. Saiid and a few others were firing back but they were clearly taken by surprise. Like 'Call of Duty' but without unlimited lives and unlimited ammo.

And I wasn't the only one. We got out of the main square but were still in a firefight. Ahead of me, I saw a teenager practically knock over a man who was also running. It was hard to miss those ear lobes, swinging.

I ducked into an alley and after we got away from the immediate ambush, I dragged Ish and Asu into a doorway with me and caught my breath. Ish and Asu were crying and shaking. I forced myself to think, to just shut up and think.

I figured that we were about equidistant to the Hovel and Dad's shop. As I stood there, wasting minute after minute, the militia, Assad's cronies, maybe ISIS, were swarming over what was left of Homs.

The longer I stayed put with Ish and Asu, the quicker they'd find us. If I went to the Hovel, assuming we made it and assuming it was still there at all, we'd just sit there waiting to be found and killed. If I went to the shop we could escape. Or be killed on the way there. I swore under my breath.

Sprinting through the twisting, hallway-like alleys, we made it out at the boulevard at the other end. On the other side of it, the shop Dad worked in stood abandoned and boarded up. The door looked like it had been locked but then broken into. It was hanging slightly ajar. I stuffed Ish and Asu into another doorway just inside the alley. I squatted down and looked at both of them in their breathless, dirty faces.

"Stay." I waited a full second before saying. "Here."

Peeking around the corner, I could see that the battle had just gone through there. Somehow, the opposition had destroyed a tank that was burned out in the middle of the street. The tank treads were dislodged and it looked abandoned.

Also nearer to us was a burned out, Citroen Picasso which must have looked brand-new before the battle started. It was one of a dozen such cars scattered like the last battered candy bars at the bottom of the box at the market when they're about to order another box. All of them were either out of gas or destroyed. It was a bit like an old western movie with dusty sidewalks and a dangerous, abandoned feel. But it looked like nobody was there. I didn't know when I would get another chance. So I went back to get Ish and Asu and went for it.

The machine gun started firing as soon as they saw us. Praise Allah, the gunner was a bad shot. The machine gun sounded like a chain saw chewing into the side of a metal shed. I saw the flash of the gun in my peripheral vision. The shooters were in plain sight. Why hadn't I seen them? Asu and Ish screamed as we dove behind the car. I don't know why but I shouted: "Amir!" Then my face hit the concrete.

They stopped firing as soon as we disappeared. I lay on my back next to the car, with my head up, resting against a tire. Asu and Ish had screamed and I let them bite my fingers, crying, as my hand covered their mouths. Shut up!

The tank I saw was not destroyed, like I thought. The tread was dislodged and the turret had been blown off. But the machine gun on top was still operational, as was painfully obvious. And someone was still inside it.

Dad was going to kill me when I got to heaven. I was afraid to open my eyes, to see them dead. But I couldn't keep them shut forever so I opened them and let a relieved sigh leave my lips because they were alive.

Scared, but unhurt. No wait, Asu had scraped his knee. But at least he still had a leg. Ish was tired and scared, but not hurt.

Guilt. It filled my body like poison. Here I was, thinking I would get us to dad's boat and get them out. But I wasn't as smart as I thought I was. Now we were going to die.

"What are we going to do?" I wondered. The shooters started firing again.

Almost as though Allah was answering my question, Saiid showed up. He was pissed. I could see it. Not that I could blame him. Fatma, now armed with an AK-47 and The Guy Who Looked Like Amir were there behind him. He saw me and mouthed a question: "What the hell?"

I shrugged. Suddenly Saiid spoke to the Guy Who Looked Like Amir quickly. Fatma leaned in to listen to them. The look on her face had changed. Even from over there and trapped behind a quickly eroding patch of cover, I could see there was a volcano in her eyes.

The machine gun started firing again, trying to scare us out. They almost scared Ish out. I had to hold her back so hard for a minute I was afraid I broke one of her bones. I looked back at Saiid. He was waving at me to go in the opposite direction. Then he looked at The Man Who Looked Like Amir and held up five fingers.

Then four. The bullets kicked up concrete all around us.

Then three. The windows on the Citroen's shattered.

Then two. The machine gun began sawing away at the car frame. It collapsed into the seats.

Then one. The bullets were shredding the hatchback up. Starting at the top, they were going back and forth all the way down. Then it happened.

Saiid, Fatma, and the Man Who Looked Like Amir came around the corner and started firing. The machine gun refocused its attention on them. It was now or never. I ran to the other side of the boulevard. Ish and Asu had no choice but to come with me. They were now crying so hard, they had trouble keeping up. It was only ten yards to the other side. It felt like ten miles.

The building on the other side had a door. I didn't know if it was locked or not but didn't have time to find out. There were alleys on the other side but they were too far away.

That door had to open. Back during National Day, we watched American Football on a crappy little TV. I remembered the way the players had tackled each other. I tackled the door in the same way.

The door broke open and I landed on hard tiles. Asu and Ish came in after me. I turned on my back, just in time to see The Man Who Looked Like Amir get shot in the chest. Ish slammed the door shut.

# CHAPTER 7
# The Way Out

When your adrenaline is pumping, then suddenly stops, you realize how tired you are. I sat up and listened to the gunfire still pounding on the other side of the door. Loud fire from far away tore up concrete. Quieter fire from across the street answered back.

Asu got his bearings, then talked to me and started crying. Ish was crying too, but she was just standing there. I didn't think for a minute. Then I decided I'd better get them to stop crying. But first, I had to get them the hell out of there.

At least there was one good thing; we were closer to the boat. The sewer main to the boat was in the middle of the alley on this side of the boulevard. One of the few places I still recognized in town was Dad's shop. It would be easy not to if I hadn't practically grown up here.

Dad was a sort of home-supply goods, furniture and appliances seller. This place hadn't been ransacked as much. Looters had taken some of the components from the microwaves but that was it. Couch cushions are useless in a war. The light bulbs were missing. But it was light enough to see that someone had been sleeping in there on some of the couches.

It didn't matter. I wasn't coming back. We were close to getting out of here. I just had to keep them going. They could cry in the boat.

"Ish, get away from the door!" I said and got up.

Asu latched himself to my leg, like he was a part of my jeans. Ish edged back towards me with her hands fixed in front of her. The grown up demeanor that she liked to use was gone. But she wasn't ready to break down and cry like Asu just yet.

"I want Daddy." Ish said.
"Me, too." Asu said.

34

"Good." I said it took me a minute to arrange my lie in my head. "We're almost to Dad. We're getting closer."

"Where is he?"

"Surprise."

"Hasan, I'm really scarred!"

"Don't be," I said and walked to the back.

They followed me.

After a few months in a battlefield, the buildings all looked pretty much the same. It looked like all the brick and concrete buildings had been stuffed with random appliances and then half-shredded in a giant blender. The back of the store was quiet. The place looked abandoned. Then I found what I was looking for.

A hole about the size of an office chair was in the wall in the corner, leading to the neighboring building. They were just holes people bored into walls between shops, apartments, and offices - whatever - to get around places safely. This one happened to lead to a convenience store that was next to Dad's shop. The Free Syrian Army must've made it to get around a sniper. Or maybe Assad's forces did. It didn't matter.

"Come on." I said and took both of their hands.

Once both of them were through, I went to a door that led to an alley. Standing on my tippy-toes, I looked through the window. I couldn't see anyone. But, I reasoned, it might be just because the window was so filthy. Gingerly, I opened the door. Ish and Asu edged towards my back.

"No." I said, waving my arm behind me. "Stand over there, ok?"

Asu did as he was told. Ish, predictably, didn't.

"What're you looking for?"

"Just stay in the middle of the room, ok?" I said.

"Why?"

"Just do it."

"Why?" She frowned.

"Ish. We just almost got our heads blown off. Just do what you're told for once!"

Ish joined Asu.

I looked through the crack with one eye. The alley rounded a bit back towards the boulevard. But it was deserted. But in Homs, you never really knew if it was really deserted. I wasn't about to look around the door the other way. I've seen too many heads blown off that way. I needed something.

Looking around the room, I found a mannequin. They had sold clothes in the back. On my way there I passed a pair of commercial refrigerators with glass doors. The power had only been off for the better part of a day in this part of town. So I opened the door and looked around.

"Is there food in there?" Ish asked.
"Yea. Some of it's still good," I answered her.

I took out four candy bars and tossed two to her, two to Asu.

"Eat these. I'm going to save the rest for later."

I took a few more bits of various foods, but there wasn't very much. There were a few cans of Rockstar energy drink in the second fridge. The glass door was broken in by something and whatever had broken it had taken down all but the top shelf. And they were the only two cans up there other than a carton of soy milk. I took the energy drink, then, kept going. I took my button-down shirt and put it on the mannequin.

"What're you doing?" Ish asked again.
"Playing it safe."

The mannequin wasn't as heavy as I thought it would be. I squatted and built up all my strength to lift it, but was surprised when it simply came up, barely weighing anything. I took it to the door and used it to keep it open. Then, slowly, I pushed it into the alley and shut the door.

I listened…

Nothing.

I looked at it through the window…

Nothing.

I opened the door back up and looked at the shirt. There was no little red dot on it.

Sighing, I motioned for Ish and Asu to follow. The sewer main was right where I remembered it. Smack dab in the middle of the alley. It wasn't very wide, about the size of a hospital hallway. But I couldn't look around. I bent down and opened the sewer main. This time it really was as heavy as I thought it would be. In the time that Homs has been the center of the war, I hadn't had time to cut my nails. While I was trying to dig my finger nails under the main, one of the nails broke. After swearing loudly, Ish pointed her finger at me.

"Hasan said a bad word!"

"Shut up." I said, sticking the broken nail in my mouth. Before Ish could make her retort, Asu started crying again.

"What is it? What is it?", I said, with a bit of panic in my voice. We had to stay quiet.

"I don't want you to fight again!"

"Ok. Ok." I said and pointed at the sewer main. "We won't fight. Let's just go down here."

"What's down there?" Ish said.

"The way to get to Dad."

# CHAPTER 8
# The Boat

"It's smelly down here." Asu said.
"Where's the boat?" Ish asked.
"At the bottom." I said. "Keep going."

We climbed down the ladder in silence and got down to the boat.
It was an old, wooden fishing boat with a thirteen horsepower
Toyota outboard engine on the back.

This was Dad's big secret. Dad had snuck it in, piece by
piece, and built it. It seems stupid, I know. But that was his idea.
The idea of making a boat in the sewer and sneaking out under the
warzone, across the reservoir and then beaching it and walking into
Lebanon was so stupid he was sure nobody would think of it. And
even if anyone found out what he was doing, he was sure he knew
that they wouldn't take him seriously enough to do anything about
it, and so he could get away for the very reason that it was so
stupid. And it would work. Until he died.

I nearly stepped on Ish on the way down. She had gotten
onto the boat and looked around without getting out of the way. I
hated it when she did that. *And she always did that.*

Asu started tugging on my shirt the second I got down. He
gets sea sick as easily as I do. He already hated the sway of the
rickety little tub. Ish stuck her nose up like she was the Queen of
England.

"It stinks down here," she echoed.
"Not as much as you, stinker pants," I said.
"That's not funny!"
"Yes it is." To me at least. And Asu.
"I'm not a stinker pants. At least I'm not in pull-ups
anymore! Asu is!"
"Shut up!", Asu said, his cheeks getting red. "No, I'm not,
any more."

"Hey!", I said and then stopped, startled with myself. Mom used to say that exactly that way when we started to argue. I'm turning into Mom! Wait. No. Don't think about her. Just start the engine.

Six tugs at the starter later and we were on our way out.

"Just because Dad called me that when I was in potty training doesn't mean you and the rest of the freaking family has to drag that dead horse up every time you think I'm misbehaving!", Ish vented. "And you know what; we're in a dangerous situation here. So shut up and get us to Daddy, all right? He'll know what to do."

"Yes, ma'am," I said. I couldn't resist the sarcasm.

"Hey Hasan," Asu said. "We're really getting out right?"

"Yep," I said and messed with his hair.

After getting out of the light of the half-tunnel, we could see each other properly again. It was afternoon by now. And just for a minute, it was peaceful.

The sun was out; the water was calm, like glass. It reflected white clouds, hovering in a perky blue yonder. It didn't look like the clouds were moving. The stream that led to Lake Qattinah was moving slowly, like old broth that had sat in the back of the fridge for a long time.

"Look at the smoke!" Asu said and pointed.

The three of us looked over our shoulders and could see it coming out of the center of Homs. Big columns of black smoke rose up like menacing, featureless skyscrapers, slowly mingling into a thin canopy above. It should've been a beautiful day with a blue sky with a sprinkling of occasional, white fluffy clouds. But the effect was ruined by these phantoms. Dementors. I wanted to escape them even more.

So I turned up the throttle and we sped up a tiny bit. We snaked for a while around the water. But not much happened. We could have been in Dad's car, driving for hours to some place on the other side of the country like Dad, Amir and I did when we dropped off Aisha at my uncle's house, with all her stuff, so she could go to college. That felt like a really long time ago.

"I'm hungry," Ish said.
"Me too," Asu said.
"Me too," I countered.

They didn't know what to make of that.

"So when are we going to get something to eat?" Asu asked.

I shrugged, honestly. I reasoned we would find food eventually. I just decided to focus on getting them as far away from our house, the Hovel, the funeral, the rebels, the shelling, and the regime as possible. I decided that if I dogged their questions long enough, they'd deduce on their own that I had no idea what I was doing. The boat's bow dipped up and down like a donkey's head.

After a while in silence, we got to the dam. This was the point I had been dreading. I didn't know how Dad had planned to get around this. It was clearly in the way. There was no system of locks to get past it. It was just an earthen mound, faced with bricks, maybe three meters tall, with a paved spillway.

"What's that?" Asu pointed at it.
"That's the dam stupid," Ish said.
"Don't call me stupid!"
"Don't tell me what to do."
"Then don't say something stupid!"
"Hasan!"

I ignored them. I didn't have the first clue of what Dad wanted me to do now. Was I supposed to walk us from there? Was there a lock I just didn't see? We were a hundred yards away from it when water came gushing over it. I knew the water must release over the dam every so often to keep it from flooding and to irrigate the fields. I guess it must have been on some sort of timer.

I gunned it.

I didn't think about what I was going to actually do until I was already doing it. This was our only chance. Because the dam, gushing good now, was chucking out water at least an inch deep. We hit the dam with a thud and for a second I thought we'd beached. So I gave the motor as much power as there was and we skidded over the bricks. The engine complained loudly and started to smoke.

"Hasan what are you doing?" They both shrieked and hugged each other.

We were going up with the water, but barely and we were slowing down. I don't know why but I leaned over one side and started moving the boat along with my hand. I smacked my palm against the bricks and pushed. That got us up an inch or so, so I kept repeating the process. I told Ish and Asu to do the same on the other side. Sparks hit the dam from the outboard. I raised the motor up.

This must have just taken a few minutes. I could hear the bottom of the boat scrapping, unpleasantly, on the bottom. Slowly but surely, the boat reached the precipice of the dam. With one final effort we made it over.

Except we didn't because the outboard hit the top of the submerged section of the dam and got stuck. A few sparks flying, it looked like we would be torn to pieces. It took every muscle I had, but I managed to lift the outboard off the dam but we were still stuck. And I could feel us slowly being pushed back. I didn't know what to do.

"Ish!"

"What?"

"Push us off!"

"What?" She didn't know what I meant.

Asu started crying.

"The dam!" I said, my muscles failing. "Use your feet. Sit on the edge and push us off!"

"But I can't!"

"You've got to!"

"But!"

"Now Ish!"

Ish went to the corner near the back and pushed with one foot. It didn't move. Almost getting off, she pushed with both feet. It wasn't enough though. I went to help her and with a huge effort we came about half-a-yard away. But that was enough. With a crunch of the wood I dropped the outboard back into the water then gunned it again.

The boat had made it. And slowly, we got going across the lake. We made it away from the dam, too slow for comfort.

"We did it! We did it! We did it!" Asu jumped up and down, his fists airborne.

"Don't rock the boat!" Ish and I shouted at him in unison.

He started crying again. That's all he ever does.

"That was so scary!" Ish said. She paused a minute before saying, "Let's do that again!"

"No." I said and laughed.

Asu wouldn't stop crying so I sat him down next to me, put my arm around his shoulder and waited for him to stop. Ish, still full of adrenaline, paced back and forth in jerks because she couldn't pace properly. Eventually she sat on the other bench across from us, beaming and very satisfied with herself.

"I still want to do that again," Ish said.

"Not with me, you're not," I said.

"Fine. I'll do it with Daddy."

I didn't answer that.

Now that the smoke was far enough away, it didn't look so scary. From where we were, it didn't look like the clouds were moving. If the sky was any more still, it would've reflected Ish and Asu looking over the sides into the water. Once they had explored the lake from the sides of the boat to their satisfaction, they started fidgeting. Although they hadn't said a word, they were about to.

I don't know how to describe it, but I'm sure you've seen it. A little kid wants something, and is afraid that he or she will be yelled at if they ask for it, but they can't stop wanting to ask.

I opened the cans of Rock Star energy drink I had grabbed in Dad' shop and let them have it.

Asu sat next to me, of course. Ish sat on the other end of the boat by herself, pouting. I'm not sure about what, and I don't think she knew either. Asu held onto my shirt every now and then for support. They were distracted for a while by the pure sugar of the drink. For a little while, they looked like kids. Sitting in the sunlight, with candy, talking for once about something that didn't have to do with the war, looking content, happy. I'm not sure why I suddenly wanted to cry, and it took everything I had not to cry. But I held it in. For a second we could forget all the crap going on around us. We talked about soccer. Asu could be a first-grader again. Ish was only interested in soccer when Amir was playing. She changed the subject after a minute and talked about her friends, who she was still sure she would talk to on Monday. Asu was too young to know what was going on, praise Allah. Ish was still too young, but just old enough to have an inkling of our situation. But she was too in denial to know even that. Someday these two were going to remember what happened, probably as teenagers. And they would relive it again. I didn't look forward to that day, knowing it will break my heart.
Again.

We were five minutes out but weren't even half-a-mile from the shore. Ish talked about what she was going to do when she found Dad again. Asu changed the subject every time he got a sentence in. I started thinking to myself while Ish and Asu chatted. Man, this engine is a piece of shit. Could they have possibly made it any slower? We can't be doing more than four knots! I could swim across this lake a hell of a lot faster!" Maybe not going out too fast was a hidden blessing because even though the deep blue water was calm, Asu was getting mildly sea-sick. I started to worry that he'd start puking in a minute. Maybe all that sugar was a bad idea. Every minute or two his little fingers would clutch my knee or shirt while the small wake from a duck passed. I remembered when I wanted to be a pirate captain after my brother showed me "Pirates of the Caribbean" behind Mom's back. I thought Jack was almost as cool as my brother. Almost, but not really. But poor Asu! He was being tough though. I have an awesome little brother.

I wasn't doing much better than him, and I doubted that pirate thing would ever happen. Sorry Jack, I won't be joining your crew.

"Are we really going to make it to Lebanon?" Ish asked suddenly.

She had doubts again, not in the lies I'd been feeding her, but in the seaworthiness of this ship and its captain.

Before thinking, I told her, "Shut up!"
That was a mistake!
"Stop telling me what to do!"

She had a fit and stomped her feet. A jet of water popped through the boat. It was like popping a hole into a water balloon. I swore, over and over and over, and gunned it back to land.
     When I say I gunned it, I meant we nearly got to six knots. Asu was freaking out only slightly more than the still kicking Ish, who had to brace herself against the edge of the boat when I turned around. My heart stopped briefly when I thought I threw her off. I told her to stop, loudly, when she kept kicking out of fear this time, rather than fury.
     She was too far away from me to get her. Why couldn't she stop? I can barely swim, and I know they can't. It felt like we were a kilometer away from shore. Asu was hugging me tightly, like he was trying to strangle me. Ish cried and with my one free arm I let go of the throttle for a minute and grabbed her by the collar on her shirt and brought her to me. She hugged me closely around the waist.
     One arm on the throttle, the other around my remaining family members, I got tunnel vision on the way to the rocky beach. The boat was taking on water very slowly. A trickle. But to me, it seemed like a flood, a torrent seeping in. Forcing myself not to panic, my knuckles went white on the throttle, torturing the already complaining engine for one more horsepower, one less second seaborne, one more meter closer to the shore.
     It was now half full of water. Come on! My kids were getting hoarse with all the screaming and crying. I made a silent prayer to get us there. Come on! You know shit's going down

when an atheist starts praying. Allah, merciful Allah! Come on! The boat was nearly full. The base of the engine is touching the water, the shaft was completely submerged.

We were five yards from shore when it went under completely. I gave up and let go of the throttle. We had seconds before this became a shipwreck. I detached myself from the two of them and wrapped one arm around Asu, the other around Ish and picked them up. I made sure their faces were facing up and held them around my waist." Man, is Ish really this heavy? She's growing fast". I remembered when she weighed the same as Asu, four years her junior." Wait a minute. Asu is heavier too". I won't let him ask for piggy back rides anymore. I thought they were too embarrassing. He's gained a few pounds and an inch and a half since then. I could stand now. Jumping off I nearly drown the three of us. Tugging through the water, ungracefully, I made it to the shore. Asu and Ish were kicking, screaming, crying, yelling and as soaking wet as I was, but Praise Allah, they're just as alive as I am. I walked another two yards inland, set them down, and then collapsed to my knees. They were beginning to calm down as I turned over and fell on my back.

"It sank! It sank! I can't believe it sank!"
"Hasan, you saved us!"

I didn't know who said what. When they were yelling, my little brother and sister sounded the same. Dad always sounded like the loud speaker for the call-to-prayer. Mom sounded like Oprah (her favorite show by the way. She got it via satellite and used it to teach me English, which I'd learned badly). My sister sounded stuck up to me, but that's only because she was usually telling me I was doing something wrong. And my brother sounded like Pete Wentz. Pete Wentz was his idol, and he kept practicing English until he sounded like him. He was quietly proud of mastering that accent. Pete Wentz was the coolest guy in the world. At least he used to be.

Where is Amir? He should be the one doing this. "Where the hell did you go, brother? You stayed in Homs to help the family. Then you jumped ship as soon as it was sinking." I hate to say this, even though I was just thinking, but I felt pretty damn abandoned. Amir wasn't here. Mom and Dad weren't here. Aisha wasn't here. The world seemed not to care at all about Homs, or Syria, let alone us. Not me. Why was I alone? Wait. I wasn't alone. I sat up on my arms and looked around. Asu and Ish were finally calming down, on either side of me.

Without warning, I wrapped an arm around both of them and hugged them as tightly as they had just done me. I forgot how good this felt, hugging your little brother and sister. I knew this was sappy to say, but once you've lost your parents, your annoying little brother and spoiled little sister suddenly become unprecedentedly important. Asu was still crying. I loved rubbing their hair, messing it up and then smoothing it out. We weren't saying anything. I was too tired to talk. And it was then that something amazing happened. For the first time in months, I was smiling. It was just a smirk. A tiny little grin. But heartless is the man who can hug two cute little kids, and not smile. But this quiet was broken way too soon, by the unmistakable sound of a gun being cocked.

# Chapter 9
## Faiz

"Get wet enough?"

He was dressed in blue jeans and an old sweater. He wore a desert camo coat, tan boots covered in what looked like blood, had a pistol on his hip, a combat knife strapped to one of his boots, and a single hard line on his face that made up his mouth. His hair was as black as the sunglasses he was wearing. He didn't smile.

I got myself between him and the kids as soon as I could. I knew I looked ridiculous, but it made no difference. Here I was a soaking wet rat, with two hungry, quivering mice, cornered by a lion. And he wasn't the only one.

A pickup truck full of them had stopped and the engine was running with one man still in it, smoking a cigarette. The other eight or so were standing behind him. They all seemed to have AK-47's.

I didn't know if they were ISIS, a group of mercenaries that act as Assad's thugs or the Al Nousra Front or the Free Syrian Army. I just knew I didn't like the looks of them. And I didn't like who I took to be their leader. I recognized him.

"What's your name?" he asked.

"Hasan." I said quickly. Ish was poking her head around me, curiously. Asu was hiding from them behind my leg.

"My name's Faiz," he said flatly. He always had that flat tone of voice.

"Ok," I said. We had to get out of there.

"Where were you going?"

"Fishing."

Ish almost said something and I kicked her shin. She didn't like that. Thankfully she was too afraid of these men to say anything.

"Where're your poles?" Faiz asked.

"They sunk."

"Too bad."

"Yea. Too bad." I deadpanned.

"So now what?"

"Now we'll just be going."

"Where?"

"Back to town."

"Homs?"

"No!"

"We are from Homs!" Ish said.

"You are?" One of Faiz's eyebrows popped up from behind the glasses.

"We're not from there exactly," I said quickly. Damn it Ish! You're an idiot! I know you're young. But don't you know who they are?

"Where're you from?"

"We're…" Ish said and I sort of pushed her only a bit.

"Were from the outskirts," I said. I stood up straight and closed the gap between me and Faiz. "My father sent me out on the boat to fish. We don't have any other food. He told me to fish as I was crossing the lake."

"Where's he now?"

"Walking around the other side."

"Why?"

"That boat was a piece of crap. He wasn't sure it could take all four of - all of us." I was trying to come up with a story that'll satisfy Faiz and Ish. Not easy on the spot. "He wasn't going to make one of us walk, so he went around on foot." Is he buying it? Are any of them buying it? I can't tell. "Frankly, I'm not really surprised that piece of shit went down. He should've just kept one of the kids with him. I might've made it."

Faiz considered a minute. "Ok."

"But…" Someone behind him said.

"Shut up." Faiz said quickly. "I tell you what." He said to me. "I'm going to do you a favor. You're coming with us."

"What?" I said. No! That can't happen. "No, you don't have to…"

"I said you are coming," Faiz said. And the conversation was over.

Not for the first time that week, I felt like my heart was

being squeezed with pliers. The men with guns herded us into the bed of the pickup truck. I put myself between them and Ish and Asu. Damn it, Ish. I could've talked us out of it. But now we were trapped again. I sat on the right side of the truck, wishing I was back on that avenue, under that machine gun's nest. I knew that man, Faiz. He was staring at me in the side-view mirror. Faiz is the man who killed my father.

# Chapter 10
# The Pickup

Looking back, you could see a trail of dust behind us like the wake of the boat we were in just a few minutes earlier. The bed of the truck, which was where we were, was already stuffed with men with machine guns. We were put in nonetheless, separated from each other.

Faiz was up front, talking to the driver. But between the road noise, wind noise, the talking of the other fighters, and the coughing and choking of the beleaguered diesel engine, I couldn't hear what he was saying.

It didn't stop me from hating him though. I didn't know who he was; I didn't know his back ground and I didn't want to. All I knew for sure was that knife.

Faiz was the only fighter I knew who used a knife. Swords, sure. I had seen that online. But I knew that knife pretty well. When we were in the closet back at the house, Ish, Asu and me, the noise had been deafening. We'd waited a long time after it had stopped. I'm sure it had been just a few moments but it had felt like forever. I had heard people talking downstairs. At least I thought it was downstairs, where Dad had gone, but I couldn't tell if it was in the living room, the kitchen, the dining room or out on the street.

"I'm going to have a look," I had said to them.
"No!" Asu had said.
"Don't leave us alone!" Ish had said.

But I'd kicked the door open, just enough for me to slip out.

"Take me with you!" Asu had pleaded.
"Hasan!" Ish had shouted over him as I shut the door back on them.

Crouching down and hugging the walls, I had snaked my way downstairs. At the foot of the stairs I'd looked left and saw

Faiz through the open front door, in the middle of the little square my house faced. Faiz, with that knife, had stood in front of the open passenger door of the truck. He wiped the blood from his knife against one of his boots, put it back in its sheath, and got in.

I had jumped back, halfway up the stairs. I'd felt so exposed. I'd waited a full minute after I heard the asthmatic sounding engine pull away. It had sounded identical to the truck I was currently in. After a few seconds I'd come back down from halfway up the stairs.

This time I only looked right.

Through the arch, I'd seen Dad was lying there, in the middle of our trashed living room. I had known immediately he was dead. He was lying, broken, on his face, facing the other way. A pool of blood, maybe two liters of it, dyeing his face a purple-red. Even from that far away, in the arch of the door, I could see the long, torn knife cut from one side of his neck, going to the other. For a long time, I'd just stared.

I'd known I couldn't stand there long. To say nothing of the danger I was in. I couldn't keep seeing… that. Yet I couldn't not stare. I'd almost run away, right out of the house and into nowhere. But I'd stopped before I even moved. The stress had built up inside of me like a volcano.

It had all come to a head when I threw up, quite spectacularly. That snapped me out of it and I suddenly wanted proof.

Dad's phone was lying in front of him. It must have fallen out of his hand. I didn't know how many countless, faceless dead would eventually be forgotten in the war. Civil war, regional war, religious war, counter-terrorism war. Whatever you called it. So I'd taken a picture with it. Then I'd shut the door and left. With some effort I had made my way back upstairs, although I did stop to throw up in the upstairs toilet.

I'd made a bee-line for Ish and Asu but I hadn't told them what I'd seen. I'd also been afraid to leave the house. So I'd ended up in the kitchen. Sitting there, feeling the phone in my pocket, all I'd been able to think about was that knife…

"Where are we going now?" Asu asked.
Nobody answered. The truck slowed down.

"Hasan, where are we going now?"

"You'll see," Faiz yelled from the front.

We were quiet again. In the front, Faiz opened up a can of something and drank it.

"Are you with the Free Syrian Army?" I'm not sure why I asked that. I knew full well they weren't.

"No," The guy across from me said. "We're the real fighters for Syria. We're not tainted by the West."

"Daddy says they're helping us -- the West is," Ish blurted out.

The six men we were with all snorted. Three of them were heavily bearded. Three were in masks. They were all armed, two with AK-47's, one with an RPG, one with an H & K MP5, one with an AK-54 and one with an M16.

"Who did you say your father was?" the guy with the RPG asked.

"Abdul Najjar."

My stomach tightened. They'd killed Dad. But they wouldn't have known his name. Right? They looked at each other. This was it. I hoped they'd kill me first. I wasn't sure I could stand seeing the others going first.

I wanted to grab Ish and Asu and run. But they had, like, a hundred more guys than I did. For a second I wondered what to do. Then my muscles relaxed. Because I knew there was nothing I could do. That's why we were in this truck in the first place. The next second I felt guilt gush through my veins like battery acid. And all I wanted to do was say "Sorry".

Then something happened.

The Qur'an was sticking out of the front shirt of the guy across of me. He took it out and started to read it. What was left of it. The book was nearly destroyed. The covers were battered and about to fall off, the pages were all ripped on the edges -- every single one. It was dirty -- like someone left it out in a mud puddle all night. The spine was bent and kept together with tape.

"Slow down!" Faiz said. They had to shout over the engine.

"Sorry," The driver said.

"Assad's forces put a land mine field here."

"Ok." The driver came to a halt. "How do I get around it?"

"We can't. The infidels have the ground to the east of it and we don't have time to go to the west. They put a path through the middle of it. And we're fairly certain this map is the most up-to-date one. Drive. Go slow."

Ish and Asu were oblivious to this conversation. Asu was busy looking at each of the fighters. He was starting to get bored.

"I'm still wet," Ish said, "Can I have a towel?"

"The sun will dry you out," one of them snapped.

Up front, Faiz burped and half crushed the can. Carelessly, he threw it over the seat, through the open window, to where the kids were. It hit Ish squarely in the nose.

"Ow!" She said.

My stomach clenched again.

"YOU DID THAT ON PURPOSE!" Ish shrieked.

"No -- Ish -- calm down - "I sputtered, noticing that their grips on their AK's suddenly tightened. Then I watched Ish throw the can back, faster than I had ever seen her. It went zipping past Faiz, missing him entirely and out the passenger window.

It landed on a mine.

# Chapter 11
# Amir

I dreamed. Lately everyone's been talking about politics. Not that they usually weren't. But this time it was different. Ever since that man burned himself alive, thousands of miles away in Tunisia. All of a sudden, everyone was talking about a nobody.

Mom and Dad didn't want us to leave the house much when it got bad. But Amir did anyway. At first they wanted to bring Aisha back home but quickly decided against it. It was too dangerous for her to come back.

They'd discussed this in their bedroom. But our house was so full of holes that you could hear what was happening in any part of the house, even if they were whispering.

Mom and Dad had picked the bedroom that was the least exposed and farthest from the kids' rooms. It was the only one on the ground floor; ours were on the second. But Amir's was right above theirs. It was a regular afternoon. Dad was still going to work. Mom had tried to talk him out of going that morning.

"You can't. It's too dangerous." She had said.

"I've got to. I'm almost done." Dad had said.

"Honey, come on. I thought I told you to stop. That it can't possibly work. Besides, I'm not leaving the house."

"No you certainly aren't."

"And I won't let the kids out either."

"Right. Listen, I won't be gone long. I promise."

"You always say that but you take ages."

"Can I help it that we're practically on lock down?"

"You aren't seeing Saiid today are you?"

"Saiid? No."

"Are you lying."?

"No."

"You're always bad at lying, to me anyway."

"So what if I see him?"

"You promised me you'd come right back home."

"Saiid always comes to me. If he does today I'll talk to him."

"So for all these years, almost twenty years that we've been married," Mom had said, taking time between each sentence, for emphasis I guess. "You've said we were different, that I had a say in things. But once it gets bad it's all out the window?"

"Ok. Fine. I won't see Saiid. Happy?"

"No!

"I can't please you, can I!?"

"You can please me by staying here."

"This conversation is going nowhere and it shouldn't be happening anyway."

They were quiet for a minute.

"Have you heard from your brother in Damascus?"

"Yes." Dad had replied, in a completely different tone of voice. "No word yet."

"It's been six days…"

"Four hours, twenty…" He'd stopped for a minute I think to look at his cell phone, "three minutes…"

"She's gone isn't she?"

"Aisha will turn up. I promise. Assad's been releasing protestors."

"Not all of them."

"But he releases most of the women. Right?" Dad had said.

"I guess."

"We should've never let her go to college in Damascus. It's dangerous out there."

"So why are you going?"

"I just told you!" Dad whispered. "Now enough. I've got to go."

"You're just as likely to die as I am. Then what will I do?"

Dad left.

Amir and I had been very quiet while we'd listened to this. We listened for another minute as Mom sighed and stood up. We heard her walk over to the dresser and slam a drawer shut. Dad always left them open. So did Amir and I. Mom didn't like it. Amir didn't like what he heard next.

Mom was crying.

He lay back on his bed, took out his iPod so he didn't have to listen to it, and opened a magazine about an American rock band. I looked around his bedroom. It was a small, narrow room with a bed and a dresser taking up one wall, a rug taking up the rest of the floor, a few lamps, posters of American and European bands on the wall and an ancient computer next to the window.

I spun around in the second-hand office chair Dad had brought back from the office and went back online. Mohammed Bouazizi was big news even in America. I was reading the New York Times Arabic webpage about him.

Bouazizi was a Tunisian street vendor who was embarrassed in some way by the police. So he went to the local municipal office in his town, Ben Arouse, and set himself on fire. A few days later he died. I wondered if he was why my sister was gone...

# Chapter 12

## Into A Mine Field

Then it all changed. Have you ever sat on a washing machine while it was running? The whole world shook, almost like that. I woke up.

"Hasan!"
"Hasan!"
"Hasan!"
"Hasan!"
"Hasan!"

For two people so small, it was amazing how hard they could shake me. I sat up and my peripherals went fuzzy. Ish and Asu were crying violently and trying to stand me up. But I weighed too much. I sat up and slowly, began to take the world in.

The pickup was on its side. Where the land mine had been, a fire now burned inside a small crater. Oils of different colors were spilling out of the engine and underbelly onto the ground. The odd thing was that besides the fire, it was all fine.

I mean, it was a beautiful day. Is this what the world saw? If you ignored the truck, and us, and Homs, the sun was out, the sky was blue, it was warm, what few clouds were there were white and innocent-looking. Is this what the world saw? It was nice. No wonder they ignored Syria. I was tempted to join them, for a moment.

But Ish would have none of that. She hit my shoulder again. I looked at her. Ish's hair was a mess, her shirt was torn and had fallen down again; the fear of hell was in her eyes, and the eyes were crying.

"Ok", I thought." The empty can must've hit a land mine or something. It's amazing that we're still alive. Praise Allah! That's so stupidly improbable. We've got to get out of here somehow."

"Are you guys alright?" I asked.

57

They spoke on top of each other and were crying so hard I couldn't understand them. Getting to my feet, I held both of their hands and looked around. Petrol was leaking out of the pickup slowly. It was getting too close to the fire for my taste so I decided that we had to leave. But before I did I stopped in my tracks. We were still in a land mine field.

"Where did the other guys go?"
"They followed the tracks," Ish pointed.

Of course. We had to get going. Before we left, I bent down and cleaned Ish's face, and then Asu's. The cut on Ish's face was just a scratch. She hadn't even noticed it until I pointed it out. But I had to check it four times before I convinced myself it was just a cut.

"LISTEN TO ME!" Asu shrieked. He had been talking this whole time but I have no idea what he was saying.
"What?" Ish and I asked him at once.
"Listen to me or I'm going to go!"
"No!" Ish was not having it. She grabbed his arm. "Don't you dare freaking leave us! Just say here! Do as you are told!"
"No!"
I intervened. "Asu, Asu. C'mere."
He got Ish to let go of him and he hugged me and cried. Ish and I were quiet for a minute.
"Are we going to follow the tracks too?" Ish finally asked.
"Yep."    I looked down. "Hey, Asu."
"Yea?" He looked up at me.
"Want a piggy-back ride?"

This was exactly what Asu needed to hear. Not that he's very old, but he seemed to lose several years in as many seconds. He was a kid again! I couldn't resist hugging him as I picked him up and he crawled onto my back. Ish dusted herself off while we did this, and we both looked back at the tracks. We couldn't see anyone. I couldn't help but think of a balancing beam.

"So we're going to follow the tracks like they did?" asked

Ish.

"I can't think of anything else to do," I said.

"Yea. You're probably right."

"Ready?"

"Ready," Ish said and took my hand.

"Ready!" Asu said, reminding me somehow of a dog ready for a long drive.  We set off.

# Chapter 13
# Balancing Beam

I felt like I had been run over. After swimming and being thrown off a truck by an explosion, part of me wanted to give up. But I didn't.

I didn't so much hold hands with Ish as I just latched on. I would weld our hands together if I could. This wasn't like not wanting them to wander off at home. If they wander off here, and made one wrong step, I'll be scraping them off the ground with a shovel.

"Let's go." I said.

Ok. The tire tracks were relatively visible, they were so new. I stayed in-between the tracks, and for a few minutes, we just walked. It's only when it's this silent, that you notice how loud the world is. There weren't any particular noises, just our feet crunching on the ground. Almost like there's snow on it. But it's just dirt. And blood.

I thought about walking in front of Ish. But I decided that if we did hit another mine, it wouldn't matter who was going first. So I just made sure Ish remembered to walk on the actual tire tread, and stay there.

At least I was satisfied to have Asu riding on my shoulders. If he had scampered off I was sure he would hit a mine, and then I would really be in for it with Dad. He fell asleep immediately.

"Marching must be like this," Ish said after a while.
"How so?"
"Well. It's hot. We're in the middle of nowhere. My feet hurt. I'm hungry, and I have no idea where we're going."
I laugh a bit. "We're going to Lebanon."
"Maybe we shouldn't."
"What do you mean?"

"Dad is going to be really mad when he finds out that you let us get picked up by strangers in a pickup truck and they drove into a landmine field."

"Oh…" For a second I thought she meant she didn't want me in charge or something. But now, I'd rather she thought that, than know the truth. "I guess I'm grounded."

"But don't worry. I'll tell dad how you saved us from drowning. It's not your fault the boat sank. Dad didn't buy a boat that was good enough. He'll have to apologize to you. He can't ground you after that."

"Right."

"Let's make sure we tell him about the truck first and then about the boat. I think if he gets mad and then is told good news, then it won't be so bad. You'll be fine." She pats my hand in a reassuring way.

All I could say was, "Thanks."

I shook my head. This was crazy. I wanted to snap her out of it. That would be better for her in the long run. Right? Well, after the way she reacted in the boat, I didn't know how to handle her. I didn't want to be the type that hits. Since I was pretty much her father now, hers and Asu's, I didn't want to do that. I think that's the wrong way to go about raising them. It's the easy way out and the wrong way out. But then what? I dunno. But this was the wrong place to do it. If I got her angry and she ran off, I bet she'd step on a landmine.

I've only now just realized something. Ish wasn't the only one who didn't know where she's going. I knew how to get out of the landmine field. But then what? I was not going to stay in Syria. Lebanon was the closest. But which way was Lebanon? It used to be that when I didn't know how to do something, I'd ask Amir. Where was he?

New problem. Like Faiz had said, the routes were changed in this landmine field all the time. I remembered from what I saw over his shoulder that the landmine field was in a horseshoe pattern around the south-west of the city. Faiz was taking the quick route through it. But this route was changed all the time so nobody could follow the tracks like we were doing. I thought we were safe because we were following his new tracks. But like he'd said, because they were changed so much, a lot of the old routes were still fresh. We came to a crossroads. I couldn't remember which way was which. The wrong one was full of mines. The right one was safe.

"Why did we stop?" Asu said. When did he wake up?

"I don't remember," Ish said.

Neither do I. "Do you remember Asu?"

"Uh-huh. I want to get down."

"I think you'd better stay up there." I didn't want him to run off.

"Don't you remember? It's that way," Asu pointed one way.

"How do you know?" Ish and I both asked.

"See that bunch of trees over there? They're olive trees." Asu pointed at a dead orchard and said triumphantly, "I learned about them in school!"

"These tracks look just as fresh as the other one, I think".

"You don't know what you're talking about," Ish says.

"Yes, I do!"

"No, you don't."

"Yes, I do!"

"No, you don't!"

"Yes, I do!"

"No, you don't!"

"Yes, I do!"

"No, you don't."

"Yes, I do!"

"No, you don't!"

"Yes, I do!"

"No, you don't!"

"Yes, I do!" Asu was frustrated and was going to cry.

"No, you don't!" Ish was just as frustrated and stomping her feet.

"Enough!" I intervene.

"Yes, I do!" Asu fights on.

"No, you don't!"

Well, that didn't work.

"Yes, I do!"

"No, you don't."

"Yes, I do!"

"No, you don't!"

"Yes, I do!" I put Asu down and latched onto his arm again.

"No, you don't!" I do the same to Ish.

"Yes, I...." "

"Kids!" I yelled so hard I startled even myself. They looked up at me.

"Listen. I'm not going to say this again. Shut up."

For once, they listened to me.

I looked back at the olive trees. Wait a minute. Beyond those trees was a tiny hill. Barely even a hill. But that slope went down to the lake. I couldn't see the water. But I knew I was right. Asu was right. Once I got to the lake I could certainly find my way to the far side. Then we could keep going to Lebanon.

"Ok." I said. "Asu, can you walk for a bit?"

Asu didn't say anything.

"Asu?"

"He's not saying anything because you wanted him to shut up," Ish says.

"You can talk now. Can you walk?"

Asu didn't want to look at me and he was trying not to cry again. "I guess so."

"Ok. Ish, your turn for a piggy back ride."

Once Ish had mounted me like a horse, I took Asu's hand. Ish dozed on my back. Asu and I stayed inside the tracks. We kept going and after a while, I could tell that Ish was asleep.

"Hasan…Hasan….Hasan…"

"What?"

"I need to go pottie."

I stopped in my tracks. "Right now?"

Asu nodded with wild enthusiasm.

"Seriously?"

"Seriously."

"There's nowhere to go."

"I have to go really bad!"

"Well -- hold it."

"I can't!"

"Dude. Do you know where…?" Wait. I couldn't tell him we're in a landmine field. He knew, right? I mean, we were just nearly blown up. But he's five. He might not realize there were more mines. Now what? "Do you have to pee or poop?"

"Both!"

Of course.

"Can you just pee and hold the poop for a while longer?"

"Why?"

"Just answer the question."

"I guess."

Ok then. This might work. "Go here."

"Where!? Here!?"

Shit. I wish there was another way. "Yes."

"No!"

"Look. Just do it, ok?"

"You'll look!"

"No, I won't!"

"Ish will look."

"She's asleep."

"She's faking it."

I rolled my eyes. "Since when are you so fucking stubborn?"

"Mommy said don't use that word!"

"Shut up. Look, I'll turn Ish around. I'll turn around. Just hurry up!"

I turned my back. Ish didn't wake up when I took her off my back and cradled her instead. She was getting too heavy. He seemed to take way too long. Good thing he'd never really wiped. Mom used to yell at him for that. But I'd stopped thinking about her, haven't I?

I banished the thought about germs when Asu took my hand again. We walked for a few minutes before Asu brought up Amir.

"Remember Amir's last soccer game?"

"Yea."

"Remember that the score was tied and the other team had the ball in his zone and he stole it from that other guy?"

"Yea."

"And he dove in and out around the other guys as they tried to take it back?"

"Yea."

"And he pretended to give it to another player but then gave it to someone else?"

"Yes! I was there damn it. You don't need to tell me the whole thing."

"What did you call that?"

"A 'fake'."

"A 'fake'?"

"Yes."

"Why do you call it a 'fake'?"

"Because he faked him out."

"What?"

'Because he pretended to give it to another player to fool the other team."

"Oh. Remember when he got almost to the goal post and then the building across the street from the stadium went BOOM!?"

"Yes, I do."

"And it was only the top that got hit?"

"Yea."

"BOOM! BOOM! BOOM! And remember how me and you and Ish and Mom were sitting in one row and Dad had gotten there late and sat behind us because that was like, the only place left?"

"Yea."

"And remember when the rest of the shells came down, and he pushed us deep into the space in front of our seats and laid almost on top of us?"

"Yea." He did do that.

"And remember how when he realized it was all across the street? And he picked me up and started yelling?"

"Yea." He was loud too.

"He told you to get Ish and Mom and get to the car."

"Yea."

"And then we all went to the car and got out?"

"Yea."

"And you know what's funny?"

"What?"

"When the building went BOOM!, Amir laid down on the ground and fell asleep!" Asu laughed. "Everything went BOOM! and he just took a nap!"

"That's right, he did," I lied.

"And you know what's funny? You know what's funny?"

"Huh?"

"When we went to the car and everyone else went to their cars, Amir woke up and kicked the ball into the goal! We won!"

"Really?" He couldn't have made that up. Right?

"Yea! Amir won again! But everybody was going to their cars then. So nobody knew but me. I looked back over Daddy's shoulder."

"I see."

"Yep!" he said proudly.

"You should be a sports reporter," I deadpanned.

"Really!?!?!?"

"Sure."

"That sounds great! I wanna' be a sports reporter!"

"When you get to Lebanon, you can be."

"I thought we were going to America."

"What?"

"Amir said one day, he was going to America. When're we going to America? I thought that was where we were going."

"No. We're going to Lebanon. It's within walking distance."

"But then we're going to America?"

"No."

"Isn't that where Amir went."

"No, he-- yes. Yes, Amir went to America."

"Is he coming back."

"I dunno. Probably."

"When?"

"I dunno."

"Why?"

"Look. We'll figure it out when we get to Lebanon, ok?"

"Ok."

We didn't talk for a few minutes. Then Asu said,

"Hasan. What's a sports reporter?"

# Chapter 14
# Voyage

By the time we got back, the glow off Lake Qattinah was just about gone. I was exhausted. I'd realized a few hours ago, when we were taking the boat onto the lake, that I had no idea where we would sleep that night. I was just focused on getting out of Homs.

I was considering just sleeping on the ground when I saw something. It was a boathouse on the edge of the lake. At first I thought I saw a light on inside. But as we got closer, I realized that it was a lamp post outside. Inside it was dark. Abandoned.

Ish and I looked at each other meaningfully. Without saying a word, we agreed to stay there tonight. We went a few yards before we realized Asu had stopped. I turned around.

"What is it?" I asked him.
"I don't wanna go," Asu said and pointed at the water.
"Uhhh…" I said, realizing that if he'd been afraid of the water before, he was probably a lot more frightened of it now.
"Come on Asu. It's getting dark," Ish said.
"Let's go somewhere else," Asu pleaded.
"Asu," I said.

Dad used to have a way to get us to do things we didn't want to. He wouldn't raise his voice; he would just go into a sort of whisper and talk us into it. How did he do that? I wish I knew so I could do it now.

"Come on," is all I managed.
Asu shook his head.
"Come on you big baby!," Ish said. "Just come on."
"Don't call me a baby!" Asu said.
"Kids!" I wasn't in the mood to hear them argue again. "Come on Asu. We're not going in the water, just next to it."
"Yea. Don't be a… "

"We're going inside," I cut her off before she said something stupid." You don't want to be alone, do you?"

A new, different sort of fear shone through his eyes and he closed the gap between me and him. I ruffled his hair and we followed Ish into the building.

There used to be a sign on the front of the boathouse. At some point the sign had been hit by shrapnel and now two-thirds of it was lying on its face. The other third had been flipped like a book cover by the explosion and was now stuck facing the building so I couldn't read it. But it was clearly some sort of business.

We could see through a window a large room of cinderblocks with a couch and a kitchen area along one of the outer walls. There was a desk covered with old paper work. I had decided the building was empty.

"We're sleeping here tonight."

"Ok," Ish said immediately. She tried the door.

"Is it locked?" asked Asu.

"No, it's unlocked. I'm just jiggling the handle and not opening it for fun. Dumbass."

"Ish, stop that."

"Make me."

"You know what?"

For a second a gif flashed in my head. I thought of me just picking Asu up and walking away to let her die because she was being such a pain. But I dismissed it immediately. "Shut up."

She opened her mouth.

"And don't talk back. There's no boat for you to sink this time."

"That was not my fault!"

"Yes it was," Asu and I said at once.

"So everything's my fault?" She threw her hands in the air.

She kept saying something but I was done listening to her and without thinking, I kicked the door. The lock broke and it swung open.

"Cool!" Asu said. He ran inside.

"Asu wait!" Ish ran after him.

I limped in, in pain. That door was harder than it looked. I let them explore the dark, interior room, while covertly leaning on the couch to verify that I hadn't broken my ankle.

"There's nobody here," Ish said.
"I guess it's ours," I said.

As I closed the door, I looked back out and saw something move-- something that looked like a head. I looked again at the hill where I saw it and there was nothing there. It was a rabbit, I thought to myself-- some sort of animal.
I shut the door.
The boathouse turned out to be a pair of rectangular brick and cinderblock rooms. The one we were in was some sort of office. The other one had a rectangular boat space in it and a garage door in the water. The boat room, which is what we decided to call it, was full of tools. But the office had a couch and to the delight of all three of us, a refrigerator and a microwave.
The rumbling in our stomachs built up like a drum roll as we opened the refrigerator. Inside we found a few bottles of Coca-Cola, half a plate of Khbuz, chips, store-bought Za'atar, half a jar of hummus, and a bowl half-full of rather old Fattoush.

"Who's hungry?" I asked.
"I am! I am! I am!" they both said, jumping up and down.

We were pretty quiet while we ate, right out of the bowls, sitting cross legged on the floor, absorbed with our food, until the food was gone. By now, the sun had set and it was dark, and Asu was becoming very tired. I sat back a bit, leaning on my hands behind me.

"Do you think Dad's getting worried?" Ish asked me suddenly.
"What do you mean?" I said.
"Well, we weren't supposed to go with those guys. We went backwards. Won't it take too long to get there? Won't Dad get worried?"
"Ummm..." I could feel the plastic bag with the phone and

toothbrushes in it in my pocket. It took me a minute to make up a lie. "Dad knew it would take a while for us to get to Beirut. It'll be OK."

"I thought we were going to Lebanon."

"We are. Beirut is a city in Lebanon."

"I thought Lebanon was a town."

"No Stinker Pants; Lebanon's a country."

"Don't call me Stinker Pants."

"Why not? Dad calls you that."

"No, he doesn't. Not anymore."

"You used to like that name."

"I don't poop myself anymore."

"Fair point."

We were quiet again for a minute.

"Hasan."

"Yea?"

"We aren't going to use a boat again tomorrow are we?"

I laughed. "No. Not after last time."

"Ok.", She said, then grinned and pointed next to me. "Look."

Asu had fallen asleep next to me. His head leaned on my side. His arms wrapped around mine and his mouth opened a little bit. He was fast asleep.

"He's cute when he isn't annoying," Ish said.

"Yea, he is."

"But I don't think we should sleep on the floor."

"We're not," I said and picked Asu up. "The couch is big enough for all three of us. You sit on that side. He'll go on the other."

"Ok."

I set Asu down and found a smelly old pair of ratty blankets. I gave Ish one and put the other on Asu. Then I sat down between them. Ish leaned against my shoulder and I put Asu on the other one.

"Is there a new house in Lebanon?"

"Yep."

"A big house?"

"Bigger than our old one."
"Are there kids there?"
"Hundreds of kids."
"Is Mom there?"
"She'll always be there."
"Does Dad have the better job he wants?"
"Yep. He makes twice as much."
"Are there guns there? Bombs? Snipers?"
"Only in video games. That's where they belong."
"I don't think they even belong there."
I shrugged. "It'd be nice to pause the war."
"Or at least to restart when you die."
"Or mute it."

Ish was nearly asleep now. I wondered as she went to sleep like Asu, if she really saw things other than a war, an explosion? Especially in our part of the world. I think I used to be able to see things, too. I wished I could be young enough to see them still. That's the problem, I guess. As you grow up, you stop seeing and hearing anything that isn't a hate-filled explosion. But if you could mute the wars, what would you hear? I decided then and there that I had to get Asu and Ish somewhere where they could hear it. The sounds that you hear when you mute the wars.

# Chapter 15
# Encounter

I slept deep and dreamless for the first time in a while. I remember it. It was deep and silky and wonderfully silent. Then I was punched out of it by an abrupt prod into my shin. I was startled awake and found myself looking at three men.

The man in the middle was clearly the one in charge. He was very tan, fifty-something, with a thick moustache and crew cut hair that was going grey in places. His brown, well-worn eyes had a suspicious, almost accusatory look in them.

To his left was a kid a little older than me, wearing a sleeveless shirt that had been white once but was anything but that now. He looked scared and clutched his AK-47 like he was Asu's age and it was his mother's arm.

To his right was a man about thirty years old with high cheekbones and a stout build beneath his button-down blue shirt. He couldn't stop sniffing.

Ish and Asu were also awake and, Asu this time, was determined to not let me go at any cost. Ish put one of her arms across me, like she was instinctively protecting me. For what felt like twenty minutes, but was probably only a few seconds, I sat there, boiling over with my fight-or-flight reflex.

"Who the hell are you?", the first man asked.
"Hasan." I said without thinking.
"Hasan. Why are you here?"
"We needed shelter."
"How'd you get in?"
"Through the back door." Ish said.
"I told you that lock wouldn't keep anyone out." The thirty year old said.
"Shut up Aban," the kid said.
"Enough, you two," the middle man said. "My name is Sullah. I own this place."

"I'm sorry."

"For breaking in? No- don't be. I understand. Where're you from?"

This time Ish and Asu were smart enough not to say anything. I said the first place that came to mind. I don't know why I thought of it.

"Al Salamiyah."

"Really? You came all this way?"

"Yea. We're trying to get to Lebanon."

"I see." Sullah looked at the others. "Go and get started."

They hesitated for a minute and then promptly went back into the boat room.

"This place is a warehouse for the irrigation program. I was under contract with the local governorate to supply the parts. But that's up in smoke now so I'm salvaging, I guess you could say. I take it you ate all the food?"

"Yes. I'm sorry."

Sullah shrugged. "There's more food to be had. I'm just after the parts in the other room. Don't worry about it."

"Thank you," Ish said.

"I wish I could offer you something else but there's not much here. Maybe some crackers or something…"

"Nothing, thank you," I said.

"Excuse me, sir?" Ish asked Sullah.

"Hmm?"

"Would you mind if I used the rest room?"

"Sure. It's over there, next to the closet door."

She left. Asu wasn't frightened of the new men now and wandered off to the boat room. The other guys came back in.

"Sullah, we can't find the keys."

"Check in the desk." Sullah said.

They went over and looked through the drawers. My eyes

darted between the Sullah and the other two.

"So," Sullah said. "You're going to Lebanon."
"Yes, sir." I said.
"I'm headed that way. I have three of these boathouses. One of them is on the west side of the lake, just a few kilometers from the border. Look son, I know you have no reason to trust me. But if you want, I could give you three a ride."

I never got the chance to consider that question. I heard the gunfire first, the glass shatter second, and the guys die third. Asu dove deep into the couch, as I did, and ended up with his face sort of in my arm pit.

Sullah, who was standing to the side of the window, took the full blast of gunfire and was thrown almost to the door. Aban and the other guy were next to the door and were also killed. I had no idea what was going on and more pressingly, I knew we were trapped.

In the unnatural silence that followed the gunfire, the door slowly creaked open and a knife blade showed itself around the edge, followed by a powerful arm and a hated face.

Faiz was injured. Badly. Blood trickled from his temple, probably where the air bag had hit him. There were burns and dirt all over his body. More so on the left I noticed, the driver's side. His glasses were broken, but he still wore them. The left lens was half there, and I could see the black of his angry eyes. The rest of his face remained blank.

Slowly he came in, AK-47 first; the knife back in its boot holder, and the only noise came from his footsteps. I put myself between him and Asu, who poked his head out from behind my leg like it was a pillar.

"So…" I began.
"I see you made it," Faiz said.
"Yes."
"Where's your sister?"
"She ran away."

"Did she?"
"Mm-hmm…" I said. My mind was racing.

Faiz came in a little bit more. I did too and Faiz's grip on the gun, which he held ahead of himself with one arm, tightened slightly. That made me stop. He was backlit from the open door and window right next to it.

"Where did she go?"
"Why?"
"She almost killed me."
"It was an accident."
"I don't care."
I was quiet a moment before I spoke again. "And you didn't care about my dad, did you?"
"What are you talking about?"
"You killed my Dad didn't you, in Homs?"
"I honestly have no idea. Maybe."
"You did. In the house. In Homs. In the living room."
Faiz made a noise. It was halfway between inhalation and a chuckle." That fat guy in Homs? The one in the suit coat and the grey beard?"
"Yes."
"A lot of guys look like that."
"But you know the man I'm talking about."
"Yes I do."
"You killed him."
"Eventually."
Faiz and I were now standing right in front of each other. "He was my father."
"Yea. You've mentioned that."

He was so nonchalant about it that I didn't know what to say. I was just keenly aware that I had never been this angry in my entire life.

"So what?" Faiz continued.
"What?"
"So let's say I did. So what?"

He was playing a game with me. So I decided to play one with him.

"Do you want some food?" I asked him.
It was a long time until he said, "What?"
"Do? You? Want? Some? Food?"

The anger in Faiz's eyes faded for a second--like a glitch in a screen where there's a line that goes through it for a second. He was confused. So I made my move.

I smacked the barrel up. What happened next happened very quickly. Faiz fired-- a string of seven shots which punched through the upper wall and ceiling. I tackled Faiz and knocked him down on the ground. His glasses fell off.

"Run!" I shouted.

I knew that Faiz was two or three times stronger than me. I didn't know what I was doing. I just thought that I could hold him off until Ish and Asu got away. But that didn't happen. Ish and Asu came in and charged Faiz with me.

Faiz and I fought over the gun and I knew that in just a few moves he was going to knock me down or away. Ish and Asu didn't do much; they were more like annoyances to him. Faiz knocked me on my back. I looked up in horror as he caught the gun.

He lost control of it for a second when I landed on the floor. But he caught the tip and turned it around. He kicked Asu to the other side of the room. Ish was already on the ground. I don't know when she was hit. But she had been punched, not shot.

She wasn't dead, just in pain. And she was only ten. That made me even angrier. I don't know what I was before. Desperate maybe.

Just as Faiz got a firm grip on the gun, I got on my hands and knees and tackled him again. I head butted him in the crotch and that is what really hurt him. I ended up falling from too much momentum, and landed on his leg. The leg that had the knife in it. I took it out.

Faiz twisted around, the gun still in hand and was about to

aim it at me. I took the knife and stabbed him.

I could feel the blade penetrate his skin and then go deep between his ribs. Faiz screamed.

I laid there next to him on my hands and knees, gasping at what I had just done.

Faiz was still alive. But he was in pain. Blood was coming out of his side in spurts every time his torso moved. After a second, I came to and ran around him and got his gun. I picked the heavy AK-47 up with one hand and for some reason, picked up his glasses with the other. I aimed the gun, right at his head. It was the only time in my life where I felt ready to kill a man.

"Hasan!"

Ish's scream hit the air.

I stopped.

Slowly I looked up and at Ish. Her eyes locked onto mine. And I changed my mind. Behind me, Asu had gotten back up and he was crying more than Ish. He hugged my leg for support tighter than he ever had. I tried to make him let go. But he was too scared. So I had to sort of drag him around Faiz, who was still moaning. I pushed Ish forward and got us out of there.

"Go! Now!" I said and Ish went.

Asu held my hand and wanted to run with me. I turned around, my eyes scanned Sullah and the two other men, who were definitely dead, and looked at Faiz. He was still lying where I stabbed him, looking at us.

His eyes.

His black eyes.

I don't know how to describe them. He opened his mouth to say something. Something I didn't understand. Looking back it might've been "Please."

I acted next without thinking. I felt the phone in the plastic bag in my pocket. It felt heavier for some reason. In one fluid motion I whipped it out and threw it to him. The bag dripped water as it sailed through the air and landed next to his torso. I slammed the door shut and ran.

# Chapter 16
# Resting

At some point we stopped. It was the middle of the night and we couldn't see the lake house anymore. I fell on my face and waited for something to happen.

Maybe for Faiz to come back. Or Amir. Or maybe for Allah to pick me up, hold me in front of Him and scold me for killing Faiz. I didn't care that he killed my parents. I didn't like killing him.

Did I kill Faiz?

I'd stabbed him. But I also gave him the cell phone. Did he call someone? Did he have time? Did they get there in time? And if they did, was that a good thing?

So many thoughts ran through my mind I felt like it was going to break at the seams. I decided I would prefer not to know.

I was on the ground a long time. I couldn't tell how long. Then I felt two fingers poke me in the arm. I could tell it was Asu. I turned my face to the left and opened my eye. He had stopped crying. For now.

"What are we going to do now?" he asked.
I made a noncommittal grunt.
"Hasan," Ish said.

I turned my head the other way and looked at her with the other eye. For a moment, she reminded me of Mom-- especially then, when the sun was gone and mostly the glow from the moon was lighting her. Ish looked a lot like her anyway, but the way she was standing, with one hand slightly behind her hip, her weight resting on her other foot, with the same stern frown, told me I was in trouble.

"Hasan, what did you do?"

I got into a sitting position and darted my eyes at Asu and shook my head once. She got the message. But she didn't need to say anything. I could tell from the look on her face that we'd be

79

talking about this later. I did not look forward to it.

"That man was mean!" Asu blurted out.
"Yes, he was," Ish said her voice was full of irony.
"Let's kill him!" Asu said.
"Be careful what you wish for", I said.
Ish cast me a dirty look.

Part of me felt like a coward for running. But I realized at some point that I wasn't sure what I was running away from. From the violence, obviously. But what else could I do? Join the Free Syrian Army? They were hardly even there anymore. Join ISIS? They were lunatics. And I certainly wasn't going to join Assad's army.
"I just want out, "A voice in my head said.
I stood up and tried to figure out where we were. There was no sun so I didn't know where west was. I'd never learned how to use the stars to get around. My phone was gone and so also was Dad's compass app. But that also meant there was no more GPS chip to track us. I don't know why I suddenly thought of that. But it was true. I decided to climb a tree.

"Where do you think you're going?" Ish demanded.
"Shut up!" I whispered.

It was only a little more than a stump so I couldn't get very high. But I got high enough to see some glowing orange dots. Lights! I could see them, wavering like candles in the distance. Some of them were a little bigger than the other ones. Maybe they were fires. Most of them were single lights. But not all of them.
A few dozen of them were clumped together on the horizon. I thought, 'That has to be a town.' But I didn't know if we should go there. I knew there was a military base somewhere around Homs. That is where a lot of the shells came from. It could be that base.
Even if it was a town, who knows who's in charge? I could be walking us right into the army. Or it could be rebels. But who knows which group? Free Syria? ISIS? Hezbollah? I wasn't even sure there were definable groups anymore.

After a few minutes debate I decided that the last place I'd taken them to was worse because it had left us alone and exposed. I decided to go to the town. Even if someone bad was running it, there'd be someone else, anybody, who could help us. I moved before I had enough time to challenge my own logic.

"Come on," I said.
"No!" Ish shouted.

I turned around. Ish's arms were crossed and she had dug in her heels, literally.

I rolled my eyes. "Why not?" I asked.

Seven different answers swelled up inside her and none were able to get out.

"If you can't even argue with me, then don't say 'no'. Just come."
"Right, because you took us to a really safe place last time!"
"It wasn't his fault!" Asu said.
Ish ignored him. "Why should Asu and I follow you to the next place?"
"What do you think this is a game?" I approached her. "This isn't a game, Ish! Dad may have let you say and do whatever you want but you can't do that now! Haven't you seen a single thing I've seen? We're in a war zone, Ish! It's not next door anymore; it's on top of us. I know you want to do what you want. I do too. But please -- please -- for once, just listen to me. I promised Dad. I promised. Please, let me take you to him. Please, just do what I say and I will get you and Asu out of here. I promise."

My speech worked. Ish hugged me, which was weird in itself. But then after that she never argued with me again. We kept going towards the lights. For about twenty minutes we walked in silence. Asu held my hand and Ish held his. I think she wanted to apologize. I could see in my peripheral vision her glance over and begin to open her mouth to say something. Then she'd shut it tight and look ahead. She did that twelve times before we came to a road.

"Shh!" Ish and I said to Asu at once.

We crouched low to the ground. A few hundred yards away, a semi-truck turned around a corner and the headlights swung over the top of us. Ish and I half-dragged Asu to the drainage ditch under it and hid. It was the only cover we had.

The truck passed us and did not stop. Asu tried to stand the second it passed and I pushed him down by the head. Ish clasped her hand over his mouth. He squirmed and squirmed. It was five seconds before I realized he couldn't breathe so I moved Ish's fingers and Asu calmed down. After a while, Ish spoke up.

"Hasan," she said, "I know I promised I'd do what you said, but maybe this way is a bad idea!"

Privately, I was glad she was accepting I was in charge for a minute. But I kicked that thought out of my head and considered what she'd said.

"Ish," I said, "I get what you're saying. But we can't just keep second-guessing ourselves. We just have to pick a direction and go. If we keep turning around and going different ways we'll get caught. We just have to pick a direction and put as much distance between us and Homs as we can. Well, I've picked a direction and we're going!"

I picked up Asu and ran with him across the road. Ish followed me. We had no more problems on the way to the lights. Eventually we found out that I was right. It was a town. I had no idea which one. But conveniently lit was a check-point covered in sand bags. We lay flat along a slope that led from a road down to a field and spied on the town's inhabitants.

They were rebels, I deduced. The army doesn't put anti-aircraft guns on the beds of pickup trucks. They have proper military vehicles. But the eight or so people there were just as well-armed. And although they were all far away, I could still sort of see their faces. Their body language told the same story as ours. Whoever they were, they were all exhausted and under high tension.

*So's everybody,* I thought.

Asu fell asleep in-between me and Ish. She tapped me on the shoulder and asked, "Can we trust them?" Ish asked.

"I dunno." I really didn't.

"Should we approach them?"

"I don't know how to approach them," I said, "If we do it wrong they could just shoot us. And that's assuming they're not crazy. They're not army. But that's no better. They could be anyone. Islamists. Secularists. Foreigners. Americans. I have no idea."

"I thought your plan was to find help. They're help!"

"They could be just as bad! I just don't know."

"You just said we can't keep second-guessing ourselves. We can't stay here all night."

"I know, just…" I looked across the way. "How far do you think it is to that fence by the house?"

"The shed or the house in the village?"

"The second one."

"Sixty meters, I think."

"How fast can you run?"

"Half as fast as you can."

"What do you think the odds are that we could make it there without them noticing?"

"I dunno."

"I think we have to go to the second house. It's semi-attached to the others and there must be a hundred or so. We can get lost in there."

"But they'll see us run in."

"We have to try," I said and picked up Asu.

"No."

"Yes."

"No!"

"Yes."

"Hasan, its suicide!"

"It'll work; they're too focused on the main road."

"They'll shoot us."
"We're going."
"Hasan!"

But it was too late. I'd already started running. I was mid-way across when I remembered a similar circumstance a day ago. But it was too late. I was already going. Behind me, I heard footsteps. I was banking on Ish following me. She didn't disappoint. We made it across without being seen.

Not willing to tempt fate, I didn't stay out in the open longer than I had to. This house had some boarded up windows. I set Asu down in the door way to the back of the house and tried to open it. It was locked. Ish skidded to a halt behind me.

"You asshole," she said.

That was the first time I had ever heard her swear. At least that loud. But I was too frightened to yell at her for that. I wish Dad was alive to hear her say that. She would never hear the end of it.

I hit the door with my shoulder, over and over. The door opened on the fourth bang. I was sure I had made too much noise. I got us inside and closed the door quickly. I was making the same mistakes again. I considered leaving the house. But I was so tired and so hungry that I couldn't.

"We're staying here," I told Ish.

We found the living room and a trio of couches. It was weird really. The last time we were in a living room, it was destroyed. Completely. This one wasn't. It was pristine. Like someone had just finished cleaning it and had gone to bed. If we hadn't broken in, it could have been a time capsule. We each fell on a couch and fell asleep.

# Chapter 17
# Blur

I know I didn't wake up immediately from this dream. It just sort of faded out this time. I woke up in the living room. Ish and Asu were asleep on the other two sofas. The house was still empty. It used to be like my house. It had parents, kids, jobs, chores, soccer, prayer, politics, fun, family fights, normal stuff.

I sat up and looked around. There was an old Sony TV, some couches, some family photos on the walls. There were even prayer rugs on a set of shelves under the window.

I guess who ever lived here had to leave quickly. But I could tell they weren't coming back. Maybe they were out when whatever happened to them happened. I didn't want to know. I had to pee but didn't want to leave Ish and Asu alone until they woke up. So I waited.

And I waited.
And I waited.
And I waited.
And I waited, but I had to pee.
And I waited, but I really needed to pee.
I had to pee.
I really had to pee.

I lost my patience and shook Ish's shoulder a tiny bit. She woke up with a start and grabbed onto my sleeve.

"Sorry," I said, "I have to go to the bathroom. That's where I'm going, okay?"

Ish nodded, looking annoyed. She went back to sleep. I went to the bathroom and then explored the house. There were three bedrooms upstairs. One for the parents, one for their daughters, and one for their sons. This must have been a six person family. Both children's rooms had two beds and everything you'd expect in a boys' room, and a girls' room. It was disturbingly normal in there. And abandoned. I went downstairs again and found the kitchen. Ish was in it.

She turned around and asked hopefully, "Can we eat something?"
"I guess." I said.
"Who do you think lives here?"
"Someone long gone."

Silently, we looked around. Ish looked into the fridge - which had no power. I looked in the cupboards and found some pita bread. Ish found cheese and some leftover meat. What it actually was, was anyone's guess. But we were desperate. Silently, we made nine sandwiches. Everything was almost spoiled though. I threw out what I knew was too old to eat. Asu came in and rubbed his eyes.

"Hungry?" I said.
"Mm-hhm," he said and sat down.

We sat at the table in the middle of the room and ate. I made sure we all had some. I was too hungry to give them more. I found a half a bottle of warm, flat Pepsi and we drank that. The taps didn't work.
I don't remember ever eating a meal that quietly. It seemed like the world outside was on pause and we were taking a break from a very real video game. All I heard was chewing and plates moving slightly and Ish rearranging her chair slightly. I had gotten used to feeling several emotions at once. It was weird for us to be that quiet, especially when we were eating. But it was also nice. It was a tiny little break that we all needed. And in the background of both of these things, my gut was twisting itself all the way one way and then back, about Faiz.

"I hope Dad isn't too worried," Ish said.
"Why?" Asu asked.
"We're taking a long time to get there."
"Oh…"

"Did Dad ever try to call the cell phone?"

"No."

"Why?" Asu asked.

I swallowed. "I dunno. The cell towers must be down."

"I thought the signals came from Lebanon now," Asu said.

I was about to drink but stopped with it an inch from my lips. I had forgotten about that. That meant Faiz couldn't have called for help. I drank and pretended not to be thinking about it.

"Why did you throw it away?"

I chewed a long time about that question. I felt like I had to make up a lie and only partly because I didn't really know myself.

"It was broken."

"It was?"

"I bet it was the water," Asu said.

"No stupid," Ish said. "Hasan had it in a plastic bag remember?"

We were silent for a minute.

"What if the phone was just off?" Asu asked.

"I think he would have figured that out if … "

"Maybe," Asu interrupted her."Faiz turned it on and called someone. As long as the cell towers were still running or whatever."

"Or they could have just ordered them to stop to make it harder for everyone to communicate."

"Assad?" Asu asked.

"No. The Lebanese."

I tried to tell myself that the phone company must have restored service. They always do it quickly. But I knew I was only telling myself that to feel better. I didn't want Faiz back. But I didn't want to be the one who had killed him either. I don't do that. At least I don't want to do that. No matter who they are.

"How much further is it until we get to Dad?" Ish asked me.

I opened my mouth to lie again when it started. At the

checkpoint, the anti-aircraft gun started to fire. Someone shot back with a gun just as big.

The three of us ducked under the table, kicking the chairs behind us. Ish and Asu tackled into me and held on like they had claws. I covered each of them with one arm and looked around. The bullets weren't near us -- yet.

I didn't want us to be here when they came. I heard a bunch of small arms fire at the compound, hitting sand bags, metal, wood, and people. I heard someone scream. Something exploded.

I tore myself away from them and looked out the kitchen window. I couldn't see anything. It was looking into town. All I saw was an empty street. So I tore past both of them, crouched down, into the living room. Ish tried to follow me. I turned the upper half of my body around as I was going and pointed at her.

"Stay there!"

I slid to a halt under the living room window. I looked out and saw two army jeeps in the fields. Both of them had their doors open and soldiers using them as cover, firing AK-47s at the check point.

Each had a big gun on the top, firing as well.

I couldn't see the checkpoint. They were firing back though. I just couldn't tell who was winning. Then a single, dull gun fired from the town somewhere around where I was.

One of the soldiers firing one of the big guns dropped. He must have been hit. But it was about to change again. I could see just on the edge of the fields a cloud of smoke was billowing closer to the village. It took me a second to see what it was -- a tank.

The way it was going, it would be here by the time we were out of the house. Time to leave. I ran back through house, taking both Ish and Asu by the hand and dragged them out the kitchen door. I reasoned that it was away from the fire fight. So I made them keep up.

The streets were a bit wider here and a bit less destroyed. I ran and ran, cutting around corners. I just kept running. This was, in retrospect, quite stupid because I ran into more people with guns—this time it was a half dozen men, dressed in regular clothes. I stopped.

"Halt!" A middle aged man said.
"Who are you?" An older man asked.

We didn't say anything.

"Well?" The middle aged man said. His machine gun was shaking. "Speak up!"
"Hasan," I said.
The two of them took us in. They saw a kid and two children running away from a gunfight.
"Come with me, son," the older man said.

At least he hadn't shot us. I walked Ish and Asu forward and we went into a house. We went into a very large courtyard and found about a hundred more people inside. It was another Hovel.

"Where are we?" Ish asked.
"Al Gassaneyah," someone said with an odd accent.

I turned around and found myself face-to-face with a Japanese woman.

"Are you from here, honey?" she asked.
"No. Homs."
"Homs?"
"Yes."
"I'm surprised you made it here."
"Where is 'here'?"

I knew Al Gassaneyah was near Lebanon. But I had never been there and only had a vague idea of where it was. Around us, everyone was running around, collecting bags and talking to people. There were six big trucks sitting there, with drivers waiting in the cabs. Men in Red Cross jackets were helping old people and children into the open backs of the trucks. In between them, people were tripping and looking for people and yelling to each other. It was the best example of organized chaos I had ever seen.

"I'm from the Red Cross. My name is Keiko. "She said.""We're organizing a convoy."

A convoy. That was a military movement. Or so I thought.

"I'm collecting people to evacuate," Keiko said. "How old are you?"
"Fifteen."
"Who do you have there?"
"My brother and sister."
"Do you want to get out of here?"
"Yes!" all three of us said at once.
"Okay. Here's the deal. We have five more seats going to Lebanon. The group here, the Free Syrian Army, they're letting me take women and children over to the camp. But they are keeping the men to fight. That was the deal. Not what I wanted, but it was the best I could do. And they might take you."

Ish tightened her grip on my hand. Asu took his free arm and wrapped it around my knee.

"It depends on whether or not a detachment of reinforcements arrives in the next fifteen minutes."
"But he's too young!" Ish blurted out.
"We're all too young," said Keiko.

I could still hear the fighting going on a few blocks away. Another explosion racked dust and debris onto our shoulders. People in the courtyard all made an alarmed noise. I can't describe it in any particular way. It was too frightened, too animal. It was getting closer.

"You are young, honey. I'm going to try to convince them to let me take you with me. But you know what the fighters are like…" Keiko said, and turned around.

A man in a Red Cross coat came with a clipboard and Keiko signed something. She seemed to be in charge. She said something to him in French. He nodded and said something I didn't understand into a radio and then changed the frequency. The trucks started.

"Keiko," said the man who brought me in here. "I just got a call from Alhouz."

Alhouz was another town across the river. That was actually where I was supposed to land Dad's boat.

"They said reinforcements will be here in ten minutes. I don't need any more men unless they volunteer. If there is only one man in the family, they can go with them to Lebanon. They'll need them there! But if there's more than one, the rest have to stay and fight. That was our deal!"

"Okay," Keiko said, "This is Hasan. He's the oldest in this family, if you can call fifteen 'old'. But he's the only man and the others are just kids. Can I take him with me?"

"Of course. Good luck."

"Hasan, are there any more people in your group?" She scowled over her clipboard."

"No."

"Ok. Be ready to go in a few minutes. I have to check something."

She elbowed her way through people to the other side of the building, leaving me in her wake. The crush of people meanwhile had swelled, with people getting into the trucks like surf hitting a rocky coast.

This wasn't a hovel. It was more like a hornets' nest that had split open. Nobody stayed still; everyone ran all over the place at a million miles per hour. Everyone was gathering their things, looking for someone, shouting at each other, carrying personal items and children into the back of trucks. I wasn't sure what to do. My first instinct told me to get into the back of one of the trucks. But there was such a crush of people trying that I doubted I would get in. Even if I wasn't taking Ish and Asu. Then I saw something.

The second floor of the courtyard had a veranda that made up three sides of it -- the three quarters that the entrance didn't take up. On one side of it were three men.

One of them had a big camera on a tripod, scanning the whole scene. A bearded black guy next to him, wearing headphones, had a laptop in his left hand, and was typing on it with his right.

Slightly behind both of them was a white guy, a bit overweight, wearing a white and blue striped button-down shirt and blue jeans. Curious, I went to the other side of the court yard under where they were. I looked up but they didn't seem to notice us.

"Hasan, shouldn't we get on the truck?" Ish asked.
"No," I said, "Come on."

I found a flight of stairs that went up so I took them. I don't know why I was so curious. They looked like journalists to me. At the top of the stairs, I let go of hands. They dropped a step behind me and followed.

"Excuse me." I said.

All three of the men turned around. I wasn't sure what I was going to ask. I just wanted to talk to them. Before I was able to say anything someone ran up the stairs behind me.

"Mayberry! I just got the call from the camp." It was Keiko.
"Time to go?" the guy in the button down-shirt asked.
"Time to go," Keiko said. "Another squad of the Syrian Army's less than a quarter of a kilometer away. And they're bringing friends."
"Pack up," Mayberry said. "The Syrian's can't find us."
"You said our permits were good," the black guy said.
"I lied," Mayberry said.
"You …" He said, but he was clearly too angry to say anything more. He just looked away from Mayberry and packed up his stuff.
"Hasan, honey," Keiko said, "You're with me."

Kieko pulled a whistle from her cleavage and blew it. All of the trucks started at once.

"Everybody on! This is our last call!" she shouted with a surprisingly loud voice.

There was a tidal wave of people into the trucks. Kieko walked around in quick, short jerks, shouting orders. The man who brought me in was shouting his own. The men who were left behind were given weapons. I tried to get into the trucks but it was hopeless. Keiko grabbed my shoulder.

"Hasan, honey, there's no more room!"

I had a momentary heart attack.

"You and your siblings are riding with me!"

Intrigued, I followed her. She sat in the middle of the cab and I got in. It was only meant for three so we were jammed in with the kids. The truck took off and we led the way out. By the time we turned the corner, Ish was sitting on my lap and Asu was sitting on Kieko's.

"Cross your fingers," Kieko said and turned to the driver. "Floor it!"

He obeyed and the truck sped off. As we left the center, another convoy of jeeps sped past us. They were like water buffalo covered with birds -- except these birds were men with guns. The driver honked at them as we left, like he was saying 'good luck'.
Kieko spoke in English to the other drivers. From what little I understood, they were all in a line behind us going about sixty miles per hour. Any faster and I bet we would have flipped in the corners. We got to a bridge after a few intersections. This one was guarded. We slowed down.

"Hold him," Kieko said and put Asu on Ish's lap.
She reached out and handed a pamphlet over to a kid not that much

older than me with an Uzi. He briefly examined the papers, and then handed them back to her.

"Good luck."

The barrier opened and we went straight through. We followed the road at sixty again until we reached a sign that said "al-Naaem." The driver turned off the road and into a field.

We drove off-road for a few minutes, over dead fields. It was a bumpy ride. We came to a road again. But instead of getting onto it, he crossed it like it was a river, and then kept going. Kieko was on her phone, alternating effortlessly between rant-like English and Japanese.

"Where did you learn Arabic?" I asked while she was on hold.

"Back in Japan. I'm a linguistics professor."

"What's that?" Ish asked.

"Someone who studies languages," Kieko said. "I split my time between my university and doing volunteer work like this."

There were no more roads. The fields were overgrown and rocky. But the tires were so heavy-duty and the rough diesel engine was powerful enough that we just went through them. There was a hill, low but very sloping. We got to the top and then we could see it-- a city of off-white tents.

The truck tumbled down the hill like a surfer running down a sand dune to the beach. We got to a metal fence that I knew for sure was the border. A gate opened without preamble. I never thought I would see that. And we were in.

The trucks ground to a halt outside a brick building with a UN flag flying on a pole just above a white flag with red block borders and a cedar tree on it.

"Welcome to Lebanon," Kieko said.

# Chapter 18
# Camp Beta

I wasn't sure what I was feeling when we approached the camp. It was fenced off and must have been two miles square. The place was filled with tents and some sort of prefabricated housing. The camp already looked crowded. Once the trucks came to a stop, I realized it was relief, gushing through my veins like a flood. Asu sort of crawled over me and looked out of the window, curious. Ish didn't mind. I looked down at her and she looked excited, happy. For a whole second we didn't say anything.

"Welcome to Camp Beta," Kieko said, "Get out."
"Huh?"
"Get out. I need to get these people processed."

So she gently shoved us out of the truck and marched out. Several other Red Cross workers were shouting orders in Arabic. A long trail of adults carrying bags full of their lives and their children began to form lines.

For some reason, I didn't realize until now that we had no possessions at all. I left without taking much of anything, and I managed to lose all of what I had brought. The truck driver had gotten out and leaned against the engine that we were standing next to.

"Now what?" I asked the truck driver.

He shrugged and lit a cigarette. I could see I wasn't going to get anything from him. So I fell into line.

"Come on Hasan, let's go in." Ish tugged at my arm.
"Yea, let's go in," Asu said.
"Hold on. We can't do that. Get in line like everyone else."
"But... ", Ish said.
"Just get in line."

"Oh, okay. Fine," Asu said.

It took over an hour, but eventually we got to the front of the line. I liked it in the line. I know it sounds dumb, but it was nice. It was normal. I think that's what it was. I was tired of being shot at, of being chased, of being nearly bombed. I sort of relished the nice simplicity and normalcy of just standing and waiting for my turn. I guess I was losing it. I always hated lines before the war started.

Anyway, I ended up facing a bored-looking French woman with a thick accent and a laptop, sitting at a folding table. I think she had gotten as much sleep as us-- which wasn't much.

"Your name, dear?"
"Hasan."
"Last name?"
"Najjar."
"Age?"
"Fifteen."
"Where are you from?"
"Syria!" Asu shouted.

She didn't look amused. She glanced looked at him with a snide expression.

"Homs," I said.
"What about your parents?"
"Mom's dead. Dad is alive and in this camp!" Ish said.
"He is?" She raised her eyebrows.

In one corner of the tent I saw Mayberry and his crew set up a camera. They put it on a tripod and covered the whole area, videotaping the entire crowd. There must have been eight or nine stalls, all jammed with refugees trying to get in.

I covered Ish's left ear with my hand and gently set her right one against my hip. I did the same to Asu and shook my head slowly. The French woman looked at me, then at Asu and Ish and back to me. She got it.

"I see." She sat up straight, her whole manner changed." So as far as anyone is concerned, you are the guardian to these children?"

Ish and Asu got out of my grasp.

"I am," I said.

"Their names and ages?"

"Ish is 10. Asu is 4."

"Four and-three-quarters," Asu corrected me.

"Okay Hasan. We're going to set you up in a tent with another family. You're going to need to go through a physical before you're allowed into the main camp. Do not wander off. Okay?"

"Okay. Thank you."


And that was that. I was waved to another big, long tent. This one was filled with cubicles. Each one had a bed and a doctor in it. There was one doctor for a family.

It took longer than it should have. But everything in the camp did. We waited in line for that one too. My feet began to hurt -- more than normal I mean. The tent was windowless but sunlight streamed through orange from every direction. The tent had been cut into different areas. The middle of the tent had several lines going into different booths where the doctors and nurses were. On either side of the lines were cubicles where aid workers had offices, laptops on folding tables, and SAT phones. We were three families away from seeing a doctor when I heard someone shout.


"You were not authorized to do that!"

"I know," Kieko said calmly.

"I just got off the phone with the Secretary-General in Paris," a pissed-off looking woman said, "I had to explain to him how I woke up at four in the morning to the sound of trucks being started. Poof! A quarter of my staff gone! You texted me on the way out and then nothing! No communication at all!"

"I... "

"And then... you communicate with others behind my back. When I find out who, and I will, they'll be out of here too! I can't believe your ego would let you do something so stupid! You were gone for almost two days!"

"Thirty-three hours."

"Do you know how lucky you are not to have gotten everyone who drove, not to mention the refugees killed?"

"No more lucky than they are for making it to me in the first place."

"Shut up!"

"I thought we were here to help these people," said Kieko "not to sit on the sidelines and watch them die."

"You're not a cowboy, Kieko. In fact, you're no longer an aid worker."

"That's a lot to say from someone who was never an aid worker. You don't help people. You shift boxes around. When was the last time you were on the ground doing anything like what I did?"

"I'm the one giving the lecture -- not you," the woman said. She took a piece of paper off the desk and handed it to Kieko.

"You're firing me?"

"Correct."

"The Red Cross is firing me?"

"You flatly disobeyed me, risked Red Cross resources, and nearly got yourself killed, not to mention the four hundred people you brought here. We're already at capacity. What exactly would you like me to do with these people now? We're short of food. Look at the buffet tent out there. I haven't got the slightest clue of how we're supposed to feed and house them."

"So you're getting rid of me when you need help more than ever?"

"I'm getting rid of insubordinate staff who thinks she's Sojourner Truth. Pack your bags. You're going back to Kyoto."

I glimpsed Kieko's superior as she stomped out of there. She was middle-aged, middle-weight and had hair like old, crusty Ramen noodles. She rushed out and power walked away from the tent. Kieko came out a second later, looking deflated but not exactly upset.

"Kieko," I said.

"Oh, Hasan," She didn't see me at first. "Have you gotten yourself settled?"

"What happened in there?" I asked.

"Nothing. I'm going back to Japan."

"Why?"

"My boss is a bitch."

"You said a bad word," Asu said.

"Shut up," I said.

"But -- "

"Shut up."

"It's fine," Kieko said. "I knew this might happen. But I saw that I had a chance and I took it. I knew the consequences going in."

"But she can't just fire you."

"She just did."

"Does your friend Mayberry know?"

"Well, no," she said.

"Oh right, it just happened."

"I'll tell him before I leave. And I'll tell him to look out for you, too. You'll like him. You can trust Mayberry."

"But... "

"Hasan, its fine. I get fired all the time."

"Why?"

She shrugged. "I'm a cowboy, I guess."

"You're a hero," Ish said.

"But I broke the rules to be one. I don't regret it -- at all. But maybe I can just raise money in Japan to pay for this place. As long as I'm doing something, right?" She squinted into the light outside.

"No. I can't take it here anymore. The kind of stress I go through on a daily basis is nothing compared to yours. But it's still too much. I knew weeks ago I couldn't keep up with it. But I couldn't leave. I knew I needed something to push me out. This is it."

"That's wrong."

Kieko frowned. "Hasan, what have you seen lately that isn't wrong?"

I had no answer to that.

"Thank you. We'd be dead if it wasn't for you."

"It's what I do."

"No -- really. Thank you so much."

"It's not over yet, honey. I have no idea how long you'll be here or how long we can keep things going."

"What do you mean?"

"We're out of money again."

"I thought the Red Cross funded you."

"We're fully-funded. But we always run out money faster than we can gather it."

"Why?" Ish asked.

"That's the way every humanitarian crisis ever has gone."

"But don't worry about it. Maybe I can get her to reconsider."

"She isn't going to listen to you."

"I'll talk to her husband."

"She's not married. And besides, that wouldn't matter."

"I'll find someone to tell her."

"Hasan," Kieko said. "Don't. You've only got two things to worry about. One." She patted Ish on her head, "Two." She patted Asu on his head.

"Next!" someone shouted. It was our turn to get a physical. "Goodbye," Kieko said.

I hugged her. I didn't make a decision to do it. I just did it. Then Ish did. Then Asu did. We hugged for a long minute, and then went in the cubical. I looked over my shoulder and watched Kieko leave the tent.

I never saw her again.

# Chapter 19
# News Source

We were malnourished and dehydrated. Not surprising. We were examined by a doctor in his late thirties or early forties. He was a Saudi, judging by his accent. But he barely noticed who we were.

He just went through the motions just like he had done with the last hundred people and would probably have to do the same for a hundred more. Asu looked around the tent curiously. Ish didn't want him to touch her so I had to take her pulse. I just wanted to get to the tent and fall asleep. Those three couches felt like a long time ago. I couldn't believe it was only two days since my parents died. It felt like years ago.

"You're one of the lucky ones," the doctor said when he was done. I don't remember his name.

He was spending the least amount of time possible making eye contact with us. I wondered if that made it easier for him. It's like I felt that he knew he couldn't possibly help anyone. Any reason he might have had for coming had lost its enthusiasm. I think he wanted to get us out of there and get his shift over as quickly as possible. But whatever it was that had brought him to this camp in the first place still made him say that. It was like a compulsion to help that refused to die no matter how dim things looked.

"Why?" Ish asked.
"Most of the hospitals have closed. Duh," I said.

That was one of the arguments Mom had used to get out of the house. Dad used it to argue that she couldn't leave. But she'd flipped it around. She'd argue that if they were going to bomb the hospital, then they were going to bomb anywhere. So it didn't matter where she was. And if she was in danger anywhere, she may as well be useful, so she made him agree to let her out and be useful. She even managed to nag him into working harder on the boat. He was already done, but I could tell he was wounded from the argument. Anyway, they were both gone now.

"Go to the yellow tent, grab a tray, and go and eat," the doctor said. He smiled when he said it, like he was feigning enthusiasm. Instead of feeling better I felt sorry for him. But I decided to go.

I said "Thank you!" too enthusiastically to try to make him feel like I bought it. But there's something in the look in his eye which makes me think he didn't.

I was spurred by the thought of food. Ish and Asu pulled me by the hands to the next tent, which was a dull mustardy yellow, and we fell into the back of a long, long line of people, dusty, tired and hungry. I rolled my eyes. Asu let his jaw drop in surprise and disgust.

"But Hasan, Iwannaeatnow!"
"What do you expect him to do about it?" Ish said.
"Bu – but… "

Asu didn't have an answer so he just buried his face against my leg. I let him and resigned myself to put my tired feet through twenty minutes or so of standing to get something to eat. After a few minutes some people came into the room with open cardboard boxes. They passed out water bottles to people in line and kept going. I recognized one of them.

"Mayberry."
"Hey," Mayberry said and readjusted a strap from the side bag he was wearing that was falling down his arm. "You're Kieko's friend from the camp, aren't you?"
"Hasan," I said, as I took a water bottle from him.

He stopped to help because we were at the end of the line.

"Right. You came into the town at the last minute."
"Yea. What were you doing there?"
"I work for CNN."

"Then why are you passing those out?" I said and gave it to Ish.

"I'm just waiting for something else to happen. So I decided I might as well help."

"What is happening?"

"All hell's breaking loose. But not here. I just wrapped up my coverage for the day."

"I know. Believe me I know."

"My problem is I can't get close enough. First the network won't let me—'War zone' and all that crap. Honestly, it's so condescending.   They want war zone coverage but they won't let me get near it. They say it's 'safety concerns'-- bull shit. They just don't want to actually pay my life insurance policy. Then the Lebanese freakin' military won't let me. Then my old way in is being blocked by rebels, then the army. And nobody there knows anything we don't already know."

"I probably do."

"Yea? Where're you from?"

"Homs."

"Homs?"

"Homs."

"Really?"

"Really."

"When was the last time you were there?"

"Two days ago."

Mayberry's blubbery jawbones contracted a tiny bit. An idea just crossed his head.

"Son, what part of Homs are you from?"
I told him.
"Ok. Now, where were you the 19th?"
"Back in Homs."
"Were you anywhere close to the clock tower during the massacre?"
"I was there."
His cheeks sucked in again. "Hmm. Hasan, have you ever been on TV?"

# Chapter 20
# Seeking Normal

Tables were hard to find once we got our food. Mayberry followed me while I was in line but got no food.

"I have been stuck here for God knows how long trying to get into Syria," he said. "I got in a few times but well -- you know what it's like in there -- and I'm out of guides."

"He's not going back in!"Ish said suddenly.

"What?," me and Mayberry asked.

"You're not turning him into a guide!" Ish almost shouted.

"No, I..." Mayberry said defensively.

"Ish," I said warningly.

"You're not taking him back!"

By now the servers and the people behind and ahead of us in line were all looking at us.

"That's not what I was going to ask!"

Ish looked at him suspiciously, "You weren't?"

"No," Mayberry said calmly. "I actually just wanted an interview."

"An interview?"

"Sure. We can download videos online and cover the bureaucrat talk and analyze the statistics of the war into the ground. But you -- you're a teenager and you've been in the war. You guys. The most impressionable, most vulnerable. The last ones who should see anything like this. But you have. Now I want to talk about your story. Not just another bombing report that sounds like every other one or another shouting match between the battling sides on the news."

The three of us were quiet for a minute. We edged sideways and another aid worker plopped three scoopfuls of who-knows-what on our plastic trays. My brain was digesting the suggestion and I'm sure Ish's and Asu's were too.

"Maybe..." Ish and I said at once.

"Thanks," Mayberry shook my hand. "Just promise me you'll think about it."

"Ok."

I've never thought harder than I did as Mayberry walked away to distribute more water. Ish and Asu stepped on either side of me as I walked towards the emptier tables on the premise of finding a place to eat. But my brain wouldn't stop thinking. Steps became harder and harder as my brain siphoned off more power to think. Eventually it became loud white noise where I couldn't decipher my own thoughts. It reached critical mass and popped.

"Why not?" I thought. I didn't have much to lose. I suddenly made up my mind. I turned around and shouted.

"I'll do it!"

"Yes, "I'll do it."

# Chapter 21
# School Scene.

I woke up stiff, like I was the Tin Man in The Wizard of Oz, caught in a hurricane. It took me five minutes to crack and work my ligaments out so I could stand up. We were sharing a tent with another family.

A short time before, the three of us had eaten like pigs and a family of five sat next to us-- a harried married couple with three kids. One of them was a girl who was my age. I think she was shell-shocked and didn't want to look at anything except her plate and her mom's shoulder that she buried her face into every now and then. She had two brothers about Asu's age. They tried talking to me and Ish.

"Where are you from?"one of them ventured.
"Homs," said Ish.
"When did you leave?"
"Two days ago."
"That was when…," the second kid said, then stopped.

He must've realized that was when the clock tower massacre happened, and decided not to say anything. So he just focused on eating, afraid of offending us or bringing back terrible memories. I decided to let him. After an awkward pause, the father, Ibrahim, addressed me.

"Son, I have secured a tent with four extra spaces. The three of you are welcome to share it."
"Thank you!" I said so quickly I forgot to swallow and almost spat food out.

They were gone now. I almost woke up Ish and Asu up but then decided against it. I felt like they deserved to sleep forever. I cracked my back and stood just outside the entrance to the tent. The midmorning sun had shown, inappropriately cheery, over the camp. Hundreds of identical igloo-shaped tents stood like zits on a teenagers' face, along the Lebanese countryside.

The camp was on a low, sloping hill between the border and Hermel. Just a bit downhill, the Al Assi River was dribbling along like a long, unraveled string of spaghetti back towards Syria.

The river was the only side of the camp that didn't have a ten-meter high, chain-link fence with razor wire around it. I was halfway from the top of the small, barren hill where the big cafeteria tent Kieko was fired in sat. There must have been several thousand people in this camp. My tent was one of countless tents in a grid like hundreds of camps in Lebanon, Turkey, Jordan and Iraq up until recently.

People were milling about, loitering, talking to each other and picking up trash. A couple of families more optimistic than me had dug little rows to plant seeds for a garden. But this hill was semi-desert, like broken-up concrete, so I couldn't see the garden ever growing. A few people were carrying bags back from the aid station. A few others were using tools to improve what we were given but most of them seemed to be looking around like I was, thinking "Now what?"

The difference was I had a decision to make. Should I do the interview for Mayberry or not? I was conflicted. I'd initially said 'yes'. But then something else occurred to me-- the image of Aisha screaming, blood splattering on or out of her-- and I decided I couldn't. Even if she hadn't been hit, she had probably been killed right after. However, I didn't want to think so. And if that was true, she had to be in jail. The police had been so close they must have gotten her. If that was the case, then I definitely couldn't go on TV. If they figured out I was her brother they could take it out on her.

But what about Mom? What about Dad? They couldn't be hurt now. And I wanted to speak for them. I have no idea how many people have died. What's the point of making it out, of surviving, or of fighting if you are never going to tell the rest of the world? What about Amir? Assuming he was still alive, he must have been wondering what happened to us. Why not tell him?

"Hasan, I'm hungry," Asu said.
I didn't hear him and he startled me. I turned around and

picked him up. "Me, too."

We woke up Ish and took her down to the canteen. The road was wide and made of dirt. It was partially filled of people who walked along the edge at first, in case a car came, but weaved slowly into the center by the time they reached the aid station. We walked slowly to it. Well, Ish and I did. Asu fell asleep on my back again. Ish and I let him sleep.

"So now what?" Ish said once we got to the front of the counter.

"I have no idea," I said truthfully. "I just focused on getting here."

"When is Dad going to find us?"

"He isn't."

"Why not? And don't say he's dead Hasan. He's not."

"Ish, I dropped it when we were coming here, but now is the time to tell you. Dad IS dead. Just like Mom."

"Don't talk about Mom. It's too soon."

"Ish… "

"And don't you dare think that my promise to do what you said included my own mind Hasan. My brain is MY brain and I will think whatever I want. Do what you want to me but you will never change my mind. And don't say that I'm a little girl and I should do what I am told. The whole point of this revolution is to reject that kind of thinking! Isn't it? Assad wants to just control autocratically. He wants everyone in their place. Let me think just like everyone else! I am going to believe whatever I want to believe."

"Fair enough, but you have to listen to the truth when it's in your face."

"Why do you keep holding onto this fantasy that Dad's dead? Why can't you just be     happy he's alive?"

"He's not, Ish."

"Prove it."

I didn't say anything.

"Prove it," She said.

"I can't."
"Why not?"
"Faiz has my phone."
"What? What do you mean?"
"After Faiz tried to kill us in that house, I threw my cell phone at him. The picture of Dad's body was on there."
"Why did you do that? Why did you give him a way to call help?"
"He was dying."
"Exactly!"
"Yes -- exactly."

That shut her up a minute.

"So the picture was on the phone?," She glossed over what I'd done.
"Uh-huh."
"How convenient. The proof you supposedly had is on a phone which is long gone. That's not suspicious at all. Now tell me why you're lying to me."
"I am not lying. Dad is gone."
"I—do—not—believe---you!"

She let go of my hand and started to stomp off.

"Don't you dare disappear on me!"

She stopped and folded her arms. I could see this was not going anywhere. I felt like I had no control over her, like she could just disappear as quickly as Mom had, as Saiid had, as Amir had, as Faiz had.

"Can we just go eat?"
Ish turned around and looked at my shoes. "Yea, fine."

I felt like I wasn't a real replacement for Dad as the head of the family. I was the oldest, the oldest that was left anyway, but I had no authority over them--especially not over Ish. But she took my hand again and let me lead her into the tent. The proof would come to her years from now when she realized eventually that Dad wasn't coming to find her.

While we were waiting in line to get whatever it was we were being served, I decided that I would stop trying to change her mind. She had to come to her own conclusion in her own time. Shoving it down her throat wasn't working.

Asu woke up as soon as we were getting plates. I have never seen him eat so quietly. Normally he is all over the place-- spilling half of the food off his spoon, not closing his mouth entirely, talking while he was eating, making a joke, burping , then saying 'Sorry', then burping again, louder this time, joyfully joking and messing around, twisting around on his seat and even standing up on it, laughing between bites. But not today, not this time. He barely said a word. He just ate mechanically, like a ventriloquist dummy. It freaked me out, but I didn't know how to fix him, or if I wanted to, even if I could.

All I wanted to do was get him to Lebanon undamaged. But I didn't know if I did. I'd seen him make more noise asleep. But I didn't want to bring it up--not at a time where he was so fragile. I just wanted him to feel normal again.

It was then that I noticed a group of Syrian adults and aid workers, including the woman who fired Kieko, gathering up children. A father was walking his children past us and I said:

"Excuse me? What're they doing?"
"School."
"School?"
"Yes," the man said, "the aid group has been here for three months so they've started a temporary school."

He moved his children along and I glanced sideways at Ish. What struck me wasn't just the kids, but also the man. Maybe it was selfish of me but HE looked happier than they did. Kids going to school. It was normal.

"No," She said.
I nodded.
"No!"
I smiled. "Yes."

"I don't want to go to school!"

"I do," Asu said.

"Come on Ish, two against one."

"But… "

Ignoring her coming protest, I took the two of them by the hand to the trailer that they had converted into a school room. This was great! Just what they needed. I wasn't going, but they were.

They deserved this.

They were finally going to do something normal. School was a tiny little off-white shack with probably nothing in it but a dry erase board and some markers. But I didn't care. I didn't care what they learned or talked about. I had no idea how good the classes actually were but decided they were better than nothing. They could just doodle for all I cared. I wanted them to go to school and hate having to go to school like every other kid in the world. Suddenly what I thought had been so unfair seemed like such a privilege and I couldn't wait to drag them there and throw them in.

At the door to the trailer was a fussy-looking mustached man wearing a thawb, and holding a clip board.

"I take it you're in charge of these kids?," he said without preamble.

"I'm the head of the family, yes sir."

He shook his head. "Shame. I'm sorry you lost your parents."

"How do you know…?" Asu began.

"I've seen it a million times now. Is it just them or are you attending too?"

"How much does it cost?"

"It's free."

"Free?"

"For the time being," He said in a Turkish accent. "That might change when the money runs out. It always does in these operations. I've been with Save the Children for fifteen years. Always happens."

"Just them then."

"But!" Ish and Asu said at once.

"Just them."

"But what are you going to do?" Asu asked.

"I'm going to look for a job. Ibrahim said there was this and that to do around camp."

"But... "

"The point is I can work.  You can't."

"Yes, I can!" Ish said.

"Can't."

"Can."

"Can't."

"Can.

"Can't."

The Turkish man looked more annoyed than ever.

"Mom wanted you to go to college!"

She had said that all my life. But I hadn't thought about that for a long time.

"What?"

"You heard me. How are you going to do that if you're not going to go to school?"

I squatted down next to her. "I dunno."
I mostly wanted to end our newest argument to get her in there. I said, "I don't know and maybe I will some day. But listen: You are all that matters now. I don't care if I go to college or anything like that. Maybe I will. But all that matters to me is that you and Asu get something resembling normal in life. That starts here. It's the best shot you've got and you're taking it."

"But..."

" ...And you can't go to school with an empty stomach. I don't know how long the food aid will last any more than you or Kieko do. So I'm going to work to make sure we're all right. If we are here for a while, then I'll join you. Meantime, I need you to go and take care of Asu in there. Ok?"

She was quiet for a long time. "Fine."

Ish grudgingly hugged me and then left and introduced herself to a pair of girls by the door. They started talking immediately and I heard the three of them laugh about something when Asu tugged my shirt.

"You're coming in, right?" he asked.
"No."
"Come in with me. Please."
" I can't."
"Why not?"

I dropped to one knee again. "Asu, I know you've been through a lot lately. But sooner or later you have to take a deep breath and spend a few hours away from me, okay?"
"No."
"Don't cry. Be a big boy for me, ok? Asu -- you have been through more than anybody. I know you have. But you don't have to anymore. It's not perfect but it's' normal'. It's a safe place away from all the fighting where you can just be a kid again -- a kid. I want that for you. You deserve it. Now give me a hug and go inside. I don't even think they have books or anything, so you'll just be drawing or something. You like to draw, remember?"

Asu looked at me, wiped his eyes and nodded. He hugged me and followed Ish and her new friends inside.

# Chapter 22
# "Live from Lebanon..."

Walking around the camp, I couldn't stop smiling. It hadn't occurred to me until just then, but I was so pleased with myself as I walked away. The world, ours at least, had been turned inside out but at last, finally it wasn't. I'd found something normal -- going to school. And I jumped at it, even if it wasn't for me.

It turned out that there was a labor shortage in town. There were lots of hands-on, simple jobs. They were building a city from scratch. I could be a laborer, a plumber's assistant, an electrician, an electrician's assistant, a mover, a janitor; I could work on the food line.

I couldn't decide what I wanted to do so I decided to leave applications everywhere. I would be making the money from now on, and ended up working the second I applied at my first stop.

A new shipment of supplies arrived. Fuel, blankets, medical supplies, new clothes, toiletries, new building materials. It all had to be unloaded and they paid me pretty well for two hours work. After that I walked back to the school.

The kids were out playing in a square of dirt immediately outside the school. It looked like most of them were using the compound as a massive hiding ground for tag.

I sat in the shadows of one tent and just watched them. Asu was it. While slower than just about everybody else in the school, he was maneuverable if nothing else. He got a boy twice as tall as him as soon as I sat down, and then scampered off. Unexpectedly, I felt like crying. I was about to when I got company.

"Hey, Hasan," a familiar voice said.
I looked over my shoulder, "Mayberry."
"You ok, son?"
"I'm fine," I said, but he knew I was lying.
He sat down next to me. "How's business?"
"I made some money today. I have applications

everywhere."

"So does every refugee in camp."

"I know. But I had to try, right?"

"I guess." I looked at his hands, which he had held together. I knew what he was going to bring up.

"The answer is 'no'."

"I was trying to engage in polite chit-chat before I asked."

"I know. And I appreciate the offer, but 'no'."

"May I ask why?"

I told him about Amir and Aisha.

"And furthermore, your job strikes me as more than a little opportunistic."

"You mean my job is to video-tape and use the misfortunes of other people for ratings?"

"Something like that. I know you're just doing your job."

"Would you rather nobody in the world knew about all this?"

"No." I didn't know why I was suddenly angry. "But it's the way the West does it. It never bothered me before but it does all of a sudden."

"I get what you're saying. But I would like to make a counter-argument if I may mess with your emotions for a minute."

"Go on."

"Your mom and dad. Possibly your sister. Your friends. They're gone and there's nothing you can do about it. So why not give them a voice?"

"Yea, why not give them a voice?"

"You said your brother and sister deserve this," he gestured to the school, "so don't your family and friends deserve to have their story told? Don't the people in your country deserve somebody to stand up for them?"

"You want that to be me?"

"Hasan -- I didn't pick you for your looks or your accent. You're smart. I can tell. I could ask anybody in this camp for a story and they'd all say, 'It's pretty bad.' or something like that. But you can articulate it in a way nobody can. I can tell. I have been doing this a long time."

"You have?"

"Thirty years. I've been to Iraq, Afghanistan, Rwanda, the DRC, the CAR, Sri Lanka, eastern Burma, Yugoslavia, the cartels in Rio, Sao Paulo, Bogotá, Meidien, Caracas, Juarez, Mexico City, South Chicago, Detroit. Everywhere. After this, they're probably going to ship me to the Ukraine."

"Why?"

"That's what they do. They ship me from one crisis to another to do something resembling in-depth reporting. Not many other reporters will jump into war zones as quickly as I will AND come back with usable material."

"So you've got a deadline, that's why you picked me?"

"And that's why I'm telling you the truth so bluntly. With kids, a lot of people will try to sugar-coat it. And there are reasons for that. But I don't do that."

"Oh."

"Who knows? I've got three days until I'm flying out. And no, I'm afraid I can't take anyone with me. But that's a long time in a war zone. Maybe the situation will change and my handlers will let me go back in and I'll find another angle. No biggie. But I would have loved to get your story, Hasan. I think it's just the kind of thing Americans would listen to."

He didn't leave. I thought about it for a second. I knew he was using reverse psychology on me. But that didn't mean he didn't have a point.

"You really think it'll matter?"
"Sure."
"Ok," I said. "I'll do it."

Mayberry shook my hand and we went to the administrative area. It was between the trucks and the cafeteria tent. A trio of brand new trailers was parked in a C-shape with a pair of generators roaring loudly to keep everything running.

Through one of the windows I saw the woman who had fired Kieko working on the computer, her face just as harried and bitter as it has been before. It sounded like she was going to break the keyboard she was typing on.

Mayberry ignored her and we went into the middle trailer. His production team looked at me with a surprised, "What- are-you- doing- here?" look on their faces. Mayberry explained what was going on in English, so I only understood a quarter of what was said. One of the cameramen waved me inside.

It was cramped in there. The main room took up the rear two-thirds of it. Along the far wall, a bench had been installed high on the wall and ran its length. In between porthole-like windows were Mac monitors and keyboards, each with a laptop mouse installed into the wood. Scribbled notes and half-finished work were all over, stained with the tea they had been half drinking.

In the corner at the back of the room, was a pile of expensive-looking camera equipment and some stools. On the rear wall, was a split screen Sony TV playing English and Arabic versions of CNN with the volume turned down. Mayberry rummaged through the equipment and produced a pair of old stools which he took outside.

"Bro, this is going to take a few minutes to set up," the guy who waved me in said. "You want a drink?"

Before I could answer, one of the producers, an African-American woman in blue jeans with a tank top under an unbuttoned striped shirt, handed me a cold can of Coke. I smiled to thank her because I didn't know if she knew Arabic. I stood there, awkwardly, as the five of them went back and forth, moving equipment and setting it up just outside the door.

I liked it in there though, because it had something that no other place in the camp had -- something I hadn't even realized how much I had missed...

Air conditioning!

After a couple of minutes, the woman came back and spoke to me. I could tell she was a new Arabic speaker. The phrase she used was a little too rehearsed and accented.

"Please come."

I followed her and found a triangle-shaped cloth awning supported between a pole and the roof of the trailer. Under it were the stools and a pair of cameras. Mayberry was sitting on one of them. I was surprised it could support his weight. He smiled and pointed to the other one with a notebook.

I sat down, let them take my empty can and the crew adjusted their cameras. I let them dust off my clothes and the woman ran a couple of fingers through my hair so it looked a tiny bit combed. After a minute, Mayberry shooed them away in English and told me to relax.

"Ok Hasan," said Mayberry, "tell me your story."

# ABOUT THE AUTHOR

At a young age Drew began telling stories and drawing pictures for his family while in elementary school. He wrote daily and compiled a journal of over 5000 pages by the time he entered college at Eastern Michigan University. On the staff of the college newspaper, The Eastern Echo, he covered many stories including the murder trial of an Eastern student. He won the award for Best News Story for 2014 for this work.

"Hasan" the story of a boy and his brother and sister in a war zone, is his first novel. Drew graduates in 2016.

## More Adventure from Glendowermedia.com…

The evil Sir Mortimer Drude is holding the great cities of the world for ransom. Only Peter Brown can stop him and get the girl. In the tradition of Bulldog Drummond.

Americans have a way of getting in the middle between feuding Kings. And sometimes that is a good thing… *N. Y. Times* best seller…of 1907!

www.glendowermedia.com